STARS OF THE TWILIGHT

Stars of the Twilight

by

MADA SPARKS SCOTT

UNIVERSITY PUBLISHERS
Chattanooga, Tennessee

All Scripture quotations are taken from the
Authorized King James Version

Poetry used by permission

Copyright © 1984 by University Publishers
P. O. Box 3571
Chattanooga, Tennessee 37404

Library of Congress Card Catalog Number 84-51156

Manufactured in the United States of America

DEDICATION

To my three daughters and their husbands and their children who bring "Stars of Brightness" to all who know them.

ACKNOWLEDGMENTS

For their helpful suggestions and encouragement I want to thank my three daughters, their husbands, and my grandchildren. Cherry edited the manuscript. April gave me advice on writing the query and helped proofread the typed manuscript. Madell thought of ideas on how to use the letters in a story form. Some of my grandchildren and others in the family gave plans on cover designs that would be appropriate.

C. L.'s brother Irvine shared letters which were written to him, to C. L.'s other brothers, Vernon and Fred, and to C. L.'s parents. Portions of these letters were included toward the end of the book.

Ken Smith, freelance writer of Atlanta, Georgia, graciously wrote me, giving me creative ideas.

The typed manuscript was the work of Linda Wells who teaches in the Business Department of Tennessee Temple University.

Others have read the manuscript and given encouragement. For all help and encouragement I am deeply grateful.

MADA SCOTT

CONTENTS

Preface ix
Introduction xi

Chapter One
Getting on Course. 3

Chapter Two
Making a Man 18

Chapter Three
Moonlight with Stars 29

Chapter Four
Days of Waiting 44

Chapter Five
Golden Autumn 58

Chapter Six
Cherry at Noel 70

Chapter Seven
April in August 83

Chapter Eight
Dimples in February 97

Chapter Nine
Man with a Mission 109

Chapter Ten
Britain Bound 120

Chapter Eleven
More Than a Conqueror 142

Epilogue 159

PREFACE

At the foot of Lookout Mountain, Tennessee, is a scenic place called "Reflection Riding." Here one goes over worn trails where others have gone years before. In the autumn some of the trails glow with sunshine through golden leaves; other trails are deeply shadowed. So is life on earth: sunshine and shadow.

When I was a little girl on our farm in Texas, one hot summer day I was running home barefoot. The sand was blistery hot, but here and there along the way home were clumps of soft green grass to cool my burning feet. The Lord gives us hard places, but sends refreshing times, too, in our race to Home. And the wonderful thing is that Jesus Himself will draw near and go with us when we ask Him to.

In *Stars of the Twilight* you will find a story of lives touched by the Lord Jesus Christ—lives that found His Grace sufficient for every need.

MADA SPARKS SCOTT

INTRODUCTION

The Daughters' Word About the Author

When one visits the home of Mada Scott on East 12th Street in Chattanooga, Tennessee, he immediately feels the warm love and genuine interest she has for others. Mrs. Scott, the beautiful lady with snow-white hair, has devoted her life to teaching others. Countless young men and women have benefitted from her wise counsel, her compassionate concern for their needs, and her unique ability to make each one of them feel "special" to her and to the Lord. For 20 years she taught first grade in Texas, and for the past almost 20 years she has enjoyed training teachers at Tennessee Temple University. Thousands have been taught by her godly example and through her life's story, which is portrayed in *Stars of the Twilight*.

Not only has Mrs. Scott been selected among the Who's Who in American Educators, but she was also honored in October, 1983, with a Doctorate of Humanities degree from Hyles-Anderson College in Crown Point, Indiana. Though she is a renowned educator, she is best known as a great Christian, a godly mother, and a super grandmother. Her undaunted faith in God, her unshakeable courage to go on amid life's deepest griefs, and her totally unselfish manner of living for others combine to make her, in the eyes of her three daughters, the most wonderful pattern of motherhood in all the world! To those of us who know her best—her children—we "rise up and call her blessed," and from heaven's portals, "her husband also, and he praiseth her" (Proverbs 31:28).

—CHERRY, APRIL, and MADELL

THE PENALTY OF LOVE

If love should count you worthy, and should deign
One day to seek your door and be your guest,
Pause! ere you draw the bolt and bid him rest,
If in your old content you would remain
For not alone he enters: in his train
Are angels of the mists, the lonely quest,
Dreams of the unfulfilled and unpossessed
And sorrow,—life's immemorial pain.

He wakes desires you never may forget,
He shows you stars you never saw before,
He makes you share with him, for evermore
The burden of the world's divine regret.
How wise were you to open not!—And yet,
How poor if you should turn him from the door.
—Sydney Lysaght

STARS OF THE TWILIGHT

CHAPTER ONE

GETTING ON COURSE

The narrow Texas trail was powdery and hot as I trudged to the rural mailbox. The sky was clear with only a few hand-sized clouds. The mesquite trees and scrub oaks, draped with dust, seemed to have dancing heat waves above them. On the left was a small rural church, peacefully nestled in a clump of oaks, with its iron water pump out in front giving the only touch of coolness.

My steps quickened as I saw the country mail-carrier place some mail in our box. Hurriedly I looked through the package of mail. There was a seed catalog, Sears salebook, a bill, and there it was—my letter from C. L.

Last year had been my first year at Howard Payne College in Brownwood, Texas, but it had been a delightful year—a year of growing spiritually and socially. I had met C. L. at church and discovered he was a sophomore in college. The Depression made it impossible to spend money on anything except the barest necessities. How my parents had sacrificed for me to go to college! We had all moved to Brownwood, and though my parents were both teachers, they had not found teaching positions. My dad had to work in a cold meat packing company. I had tried to find work at Woolworth's, but the manager had said I was too young. Sixteen was young. But I did have a scholarship since I graduated salutatorian from high school. That helped—no tuition. My brother Don (I called him Bubba) and his wife had moved with us. They had stayed in Brownwood for the summer. Mama, Daddy and I were back on the farm in Comanche, Texas.

I tore open my letter and read:

July 4, 1934

To the most beautiful golden haired young lady whom I think of always, or—well, what shall I say? Shall I call you "My dear madamoiselle," "Dear Miss Sparks," or "Dear Mada"?

I'm afraid I'm a failure as a letter writer. I've composed three already this morning, but tore them up. There are lots of things I wish I could tell you, but they don't seem to sound exactly right, 'er sumpin'.

As to plain facts, current events, etc., they're very uninteresting. We have about 600 enrolled already, but not nearly so many as we had last year. So far there are two rifle companies, one artillery battery, a signal company, and a machine gun company. They may organize another rifle company later on.

Sorry I couldn't attend church last Sunday. I had to leave earlier than I expected. I'll be a good boy, though, and attend every service we have here. You're surprised to hear of a military camp

Getting on Course

holding church services? Most people are, and generally have the wrong conception of one of these camps. On the contrary, the boys here are some of the finest, clean, squarest fellows one can find.

Please, please write me, Mada,—there's nothing I would want more than a letter from you. Tell me how school suits you, and what you're doing in the way of socials, parties, etc.

There are other things I want to say, but I'll wait till next time.

Sincerely yours,
      Churchill L. Scott, Jr.
      C "B"—CMTC
      Camp Bullis, Texas

I folded the letter and put it safely away. Yes, I must admit I was so happy to get that letter. It was a joy to correspond with him. I felt the first time I dated him that I could safely put my hand in his and go around the world.

July 19, 1934

Dear Mada,

It seems you're having a good time going to school, what with going on watermelon feasts, trips to the dam at Lake Brownwood, and parties. Say, you're having a regular vacation compared to me. We have school here, too, every day from 1:00 until 4:00. We've been studying map reading, military courtesy, law, combat principles, etc. We had a test in map reading last Friday, and guess what? I made a 100! No foolin', I believe I study harder here than I do going to Howard Payne.

Yes, I suppose I'll go to school this fall, if I save enough money for books, blanket tax, etc. Wish some rich guy would donate me a hundred dollars to go to school on. I might appreciate it as much as he would.

I'll be glad when I get to see you again, you redheaded Diana. Maybe I can in a couple more weeks. At least I hope so.

Oh, yeah, we fired pistols today until 2:00 P.M. and am I proud of what I made! Joseph Plaza led the company with an average score of 88 out of 100, at 25 yards and 15 yards respectively; and I made second with an average of 87.5. Whoo-ee! The other guys have to buy the best three shots all the ice cream they can eat, and naturally, I'm mad at nobody.

I'd like to keep going, but I had better stop. You remind me of—oh, a regular peach of a gal— "An old fashioned girl with an old fashioned smile"—you know. Take care of yourself, exercise plenty, eat lightly, smile! This is the law of all pretty young maids. Write soon.

Yours,
C. L.

Yes, I was now back in school for a summer session. The brief stay at our farm was refreshing. Nights were spent outside sleeping under the stars. A Texas breeze always blew in the evening on that sandy hill, sometimes softly, sometimes fiercely. If a sudden storm came up, as it frequently did, we would scurry to the storm cellar. It was built underground, musty and moist, but safer when tornadoes came.

Days were spent gathering summer fruit—peaches, rosy ripe and luscious; plums, pears, crabapples, berries, and grapes. Also we had peanuts to pull and let dry in the sun. Canning and preserving were usual activities and those colorful jars of food would help feed us through the winter.

Wash day was once a week, usually on Monday. Mama and I would rub our clothes on a rub board, dipping each garment out of warm sudsy water. Daddy had the wash pot filled with water, starting a crackling fire underneath it. As soon as the water was hot enough, we dropped in each item of clothes, punching it down into the hot water with a broomhandle stick. After the clothes steamed awhile, we would dip them out into tubs of cool water, rinse and hang them on a line to dry. Wash day took all day, so it needed to be a sunshiny day.

Now, returning to Howard Payne was a change of pace since studying was foremost—also chapel services. Howard Payne was a Christian college founded in the last century—a Baptist school.

In the First Baptist Church, across the street from the campus, the revivals were warm and

Spirit-filled. It was in this church that C. L. sang solos and played his cornet when he was home. He had trusted Christ as his Saviour when he was a child.

I was nearly twelve the summer I gave my heart to the Lord Jesus. This experience is now as clear and glowing to my soul as it was when it happened. My Sunday School teacher had been praying for me by name. Mama and Daddy were teaching in a little country school in Comanche County and that summer our church had the usual brush arbor revival meeting. The brush arbor was a large open area with poles driven into the ground with brush fastened together for a covering.

One night I rushed down the sandy aisle at the invitation time, asking Jesus to save me. At that instant I was born again—my sins were gone and I had a deep peace in my soul. The world was resplendent in brighter hues with bird songs of more joyous sounds—a new world for a new person in Christ.

PERFECT YOU

Perfect You—imperfect me
I rest my tear-stained
soul on Thee
Content at last to cast
My sinful self on
Sinless You.

Getting on Course

> Immortal You—mortal me
> I see beyond the stress
> to be
> And glory in the Matchless Love,
> That draws my loveless
> self to Lovely You.
> —Mada Scott

This fall at Howard Payne was to be a time of really setting some goals and getting on course. Even though I was majoring in Spanish, I also had a double minor in Elementary Education and English. To pay for my tuition I graded papers for some of the teachers. So the days were filled with much study. I did see C. L. some and it was always a joy to be with him.

During the winter my dad's health became increasingly worse. He had had what we thought was the flu, but his cough persisted. The doctor's diagnosis was tuberculosis! I cried and cried, for I was not only disturbed about his illness, but also about a recent happening.

Daddy and I were walking to town one day. He was dressed in a shabby suit that he had gotten from a charity place. We were going by the campus so I walked briskly ahead, not wanting to be seen with him. Now, after his illness, my thoughts rushed to all he had done for me—even willing to accept charity for himself. How ungrateful I had been! Regrets over this incident and grief over his illness were deep. But the Lord forgave me and gave me help.

Daddy went to a hospital in San Angelo, Texas, where he was to stay six months. Mama and I moved into a girl's dorm, she as supervisor being paid ten dollars a month. Liver cost five cents a pound, so we ate that often. Sometime we had only a piece of cheese and a few crackers for supper. The Depression made it impossible to spend money for little besides something to eat, so the ten dollars paid for our groceries each month. Bubba and his wife had moved to West Texas. Changes came rapidly, but oh, how good it was to look to the One who never changes!

August 5, 1935

Dearest Mada:

I would have answered your letter sooner, but we were so busy getting ready for camp that I couldn't find time.

I was in Brownwood last Friday, and didn't know you were there. Honest, Mada, I would give a million for one of your smiles. I'm coming to see you before school starts if I have to desert this camp.

I'm glad your Dad is better. I want to see him sometime this summer when I see you.

Let me tell you something that will make you wonder if I have the big head. Ten applicants, all of them enlisted men in the Army Air Corps except myself, reported for entrance examinations at Randolph Field, San Antonio, Texas. Two passed, and I was one of them! I think I had to thank Somebody for that besides myself. Boy, it took four days to examine us, and we found out what was wrong with us to the nth degree!

I have poison ivy all over my legs and arms, and it's driving me crazy. What's a good remedy, country girl? I used some permanganate of potash solution, but it took all the skin off—that's pretty hot stuff.

I hope you go to school this year. I would like to go with you, but I'm afraid I can't make it. We've had a pretty good time, though, at least I have, and I hope you have, too.

Compliments from several boys to you have come in. They're all three of them college boys in my tent, and they say you're a—well, I guess we'd say a "humdinger." There is nobody that a boy can appreciate more than a pretty girl who is also as good as gold, if you know what I mean.

I'm very tired tonight. We fired on the range all day yesterday and today, but it's finished now. My rifle shoulder feels like it has been run through a meat-grinder. So if you'll pardon me, I think I shall retire. Taps have already sounded, and the boys want the lights out.

Write me the news. Take care of yourself and stay as sweet as you are.

Ever yours,
C. L.

Randolph Field, Texas
October 19, 1935

Dear Mada:

I'm sorry I had to rush off in the heat of the day, but the War Department decided that I might make a Flying Cadet, so here I am trying to live up to the opportunity that presented itself.

I get plenty of track exercise here. Lower classmen have to run everywhere they go, and, boy! my legs are so sore that I can hardly make it. And if that were not enough, they ran us through a line of doctors today after lunch and we got jabbed with a hypodermic needle in each arm. We have two more inoculation receptions waiting for us in the near future.

No, I'm not flying yet. There's a lot of ground school to go through with before you are even allowed to look at a ship. I get to go up Monday, though.

We had 92 in our class at first, and eight of them washed out on physical rechecks. There are about 40 young officers just out of West Point, so the class at present totals over 120. At the end of the first four months, it is expected that there will be approximately 40% of those left. So it sho' do look mighty slim for this mister.

About the change in our attitudes before I left home—I've already told you what and how I thought of you nearly a year ago. I think the same now, but felt that you wanted to be a close friend, so that's why. I should have sensed it before, but I didn't want it to be that way. Some misters are sure dumb sometimes, aren't they? But that's over with and put in the memory chest with the curl of golden-red hair, and it will always be something to remind me that I once had the honor of being intimately acquainted with a girl who was "tops" to me at all times.

Write me if you have time, and I'll do the same.
Always,
C. L.

November 2, 1935

Dear Mada:

What are you trying to do? Break all records in scholarship? Six courses is too much for anybody, and you know it. And I'll never forgive you if you study so hard that you'll have to wear glasses. I don't believe I would sacrifice the loss of seeing normally even for a Doctor's degree.

What is the Alpha Chi a regular fraternity? According to all I've heard about fraternities, they're pretty wild organizations—you know, dances, lots of drinking, etc. I guess the one at Howard Payne is slightly modified to meet local requirements.

Wish I could hear you play the piano. I haven't heard any music since I've been here, and I'm sure beginning to feel a certain emptiness and a strong desire for a "tune." Oh, I take it back, they have beautiful pipe organ music at the Post Chapel on Sunday services. I really enjoy hearing it.

Randolph Field is 20 miles northeast of San Antonio. It doesn't seem like 20 miles, for I can see San Antonio from an airplane just as soon as I have taken off, and can fly there in 8 minutes easily.

Your family and relatives seem to have a certain yen for redheadedness, don't they? Could you sometime pay a visit to your aunt, and incidentally, I could pay you a visit while you're here?

Yes, I'm always careful when in a plane. At least I'm a little bit careful. My aunt wrote me the other day to "be sure that the door of the plane is shut, and not to fly very high off the ground." She doesn't realize that there is no door and that the most dangerous way we could fly would be close to the ground.

Write me again, please, "pretty-one-with the beautiful red hair" who shall always be in my heart what I wanted her to be. This foolish cadet will always entertain the hope of having a red-headed sweetheart.

Always,
C. L.

November 23, 1935

Dear Mada,

Sorry I couldn't answer your letter sooner. We're behind on our winter flying schedule and

Getting on Course

have been getting in all the time we can when the weather permits.

I'll bet you're really a honey in riding boots and pants. You are in anything, though, so it couldn't make so very much difference. I would have enjoyed going to the Halloween party if I had been there.

You wanted to know what we do here. We fly half the morning and go to school the other half. In the afternoon we have radio buzzer practice and athletics, or drill with rifles. On Saturday morning we always have a formal inspection every morning before we go to the line, so you see it takes a great deal of time trying to keep our rooms, desks, windows, and lockers free from dust. We have call to quarters from 7:30 to 9:00 every night except Friday and Saturday. We study during that time such subjects as Engines, Aerodynamics, Meteorology, Navigation, etc.—they're plenty tough for me, but don't seem to bother some of the boys who have their Master's degree in science or mathematics or something.

Come to see me, or phone me and I'll come to see you if you're here on Saturday or Sunday when you come down next spring with the Alpha Chi. (Provided I'm here that long. They're sure washing us out fast and furiously on our flying.) I think we may get a few days off this Christmas—hope so, anyway.

I'd better shut up and get ready to go to church. The chapel here is a beautiful one, and I enjoy going. I think I'll start singing in the choir. They have a good pipe organ, too.

Write me, and excuse the bad scratching that will have to pass for handwriting.

Yours,
C. L.

Tuesday, December 17, 1935

Dear Mada,

I sincerely appreciate the card you sent. Let me tell you this—you're worth a million to me, and the times that we've been together will always be pleasant memories. Also remember this. I'm more than a fair weather friend, and anytime you need me, I'll always be somewhere at hand. Don't forget.

Sorry about the pictures. I thought I had sent you some. (Maybe it was the other red-headed girl. I'm not sure.) I'm having some more developed and I'll send you some of them for sure, provided that you will try to send one of yourself sometime.

Everybody in Howard Payne seems to have marriage fever. It seems as if there won't be any single ones left soon. Well, they all have my best wishes—and sympathy.

Two of our class washed out today. That's some Christmas present for them.

Well, I've got to get some sleep. I fly the whole period solo tomorrow and I want to do fairly well.

A merry Christmas and the happiest New Year you ever spent.

> Sincerely,
> C. L.

CHAPTER TWO

MAKING A MAN

Christmas and winter were rather uneventful. It was lonely because Daddy could not be at the dorm since he had tuberculosis; others might contract the disease. He went to the homes of his brothers and sisters in various parts of Texas, staying several days at each.

Spring came with more joy and pleasant weather. It would soon be time for the Alpha Chi Society to meet in San Antonio, and I was especially excited at the prospects of being with C. L.

San Antonio teems with Texas history. Nestled in the heart of the city is the Alamo where fewer than 200 Texans had defended this mission against Santa Anna's 5,000 troops in 1836. The brave men were all killed after a two week siege. This was a very memorable time to visit the Alamo since 1936 was Texas' centennial year. On the outskirts of the city are old missions—some established in the 1700's by Franciscan friars. In the midst of the city flows the San Antonio River, banked with colorful flowers, Mexican gift shops and cafes.

The Alpha Chi Honor Societies of Texas were meeting here in San Antonio for a two-day seminar. Since I was a member at Howard Payne College, of course I was privileged to go with our group. Bubba sent me ten dollars to spend. (But I brought most of it back to Mama. Depression days made me cautious.)

In San Antonio we had our meetings at Our Lady of the Lake College, but we had time for shopping, sight-seeing, visiting the zoo, and a banquet one night. Best of all, the other night I got to be with C. L. awhile. It was enjoyable also to visit my relatives there.

Summer brought continued schooling as I was to graduate in August—this centennial year of Texas. Now I was sure I should teach. I applied at several schools with no success. Then later in August, I was accepted to teach in Buffalo Consolidated School out in the country from Santa Anna, Texas. It was about 20 miles from Brownwood.

How good it was to find a house to rent! It was a little unpainted house and we would have to carry water from the landlord's well. I would be riding the school bus to school each day. But now Daddy and Mama could be together and with me. I would be able to help them now; they had given up so much for me. So I looked with eagerness on my first teaching position and on getting settled at home with Mama and Daddy.

                              April 19, 1936
                              Randolph Field, Texas

Dear Mada,

After spending half the day doing nothing, I've finally decided to write you, even though I don't owe you a letter. This sitting around and just resting, reading, etc., is none too good for one's nerves. I wish there were some hills around here where I could walk up and down them until I got good and tired.

They opened up the swimming pool yesterday, and it's really a nice swimmin' hole—has underwater lighting system for night, full of clear water, is painted a light blue—sure is pretty. But it's been too cold and windy today to go in very long—it's much nicer to lie on the bank in the sun and just sleep.

Shur-r-r-re, and I know that the fairest redheaded lassie in the world must have thought I was kidding her Friday night when she was here, and I can't quite blame her for thinking such. However, if she'll just bear with me patiently for awhile longer I may be eventually able to convince her that I was sincere in saying that I love her (at least in my own mind I think that it was with all sincerity and seriousness that I told her.) And even though human beings are usually living examples of all that is fickle and inconsistent, the thought still exists in my mind and has persisted for at least two years, so I'm beginning to think that it's a fact in spite of all your "take-it-with-a-grain-of-salt" doubts as to my intentions. I often wonder, Redhead, if it's as tough for you trying to figure me out as it is for me to figure you. I'm determined that someday I'll quit trying to understand and instead will let the age-old instinct of the impulsive kiss solve the problem of just what you think of me.

But all that is neither here nor there and is seemingly "fur-fur" away in the mysterious future. I'm wondering if you found the other kids O.K. and made it home without any trouble. I wish I could have gone back for a day or so.

It's about time for supper bell, so I won't bother you longer with this apparently meaningless chatter. Write me.

As ever,
C. L.

June 7, 1936

Hello, Dear Redhead,

Since you've forgotten to answer my last letter, I'll write you again. You must be enjoying your vacation so much that you haven't time to write. I'll bet it feels good to be out of school, doesn't it?

No, I was just kidding. I think the truth of the matter is that it was I who waited so long before answering your letter. Anyway, fair Queen, I want to ask a favor of thee. You remember my good luck charm that I told you I carried while flying? Well, I lost it last week and since that time have ground-looped twice and cracked up a landing gear while landing. So if it won't trouble you too much, and for the sake of keeping Uncle Sam's airplanes intact, will you please send me another lock of your beautiful golden curls? I'm not exactly superstitious, but it does seem a bit funny that all my bad luck should occur right after I lose the lock of hair—and anyway, the lock reminds me of a few pleasant nights that I'll always like to remember. *No es verdad, Rosita Roja?*

We went to Dallas last week and I detoured by way of our place at Priddy—landed there and saw my folks. It was really good to see them again, also to buzz the place properly with the old Thunderbird. I haven't had so much fun in a long time.

The more I look at the picture of you that Raymond Cobb sent, the prettier it seems and the more like you. (This isn't a compliment for the lock of hair, but I really would like for you to send it.)

Sincerely,
C. L.

June 10, 1936

Dear Redhead,

I don't know now who owes the other a letter. I got yours the day after I sent the last one. Anyway, I'd just as soon talk to you now as anytime; then maybe someday you'll send me two letters at once.

We're getting ready to go on a cross country to Houston this afternoon and return by way of Waco tonight, so I may not get time to finish this.

So you're going to school again this summer. That's too much school for me. Looks as if you might get tired of it before many more years. I may get to go to school some more, though; but it's a different kind of school. Since the President vetoed the Army Air Corps bill and things in the future don't look too promising, I've written in an attempt to get a commission in the Marine Air Corps after graduation from Kelly.

Pursuit and Attack are two branches of army flying. Pursuit pilots fly small, fast one-seater ships to overtake bombers and shoot them down. Attack pilots fly larger, 2-seat monoplanes for strafing enemy troops on the ground. Attack ships fly low and fast and usually carry 6 machine guns. They can do lots of damage to a column of infantry marching on a road.

Will finish this later—gotta go to the line.

Thursday—

I'm sorry you didn't get a place to teach at Priddy, but you know how hard it is to convince those Dutchmen. They think there is a trick to it somewhere. Maybe you'll hit a streak of luck somewhere soon and you'll have a bigger place to teach in.

Mother said she saw you and your mother in town the other day. She's expecting me home soon, but I'm afraid after all that we're not going to get any leave between classes. I heard an officer from Kelly talking about it the other night.

The trouble with all my other girls sending me a lock of hair is that it wouldn't bring me luck.

Besides none of them are redheads. Six of them are blondes, five are brunettes, and the other twelve are baldheaded!

> As ever,
> C. L.

P.S. I don't have anymore pictures of myself. The camera broke the last time they took my picture, so I can't get anyone to take it anymore. Here's a snapshot I took the other morning above the field. You can barely see part of Randolph—above the clouds at 8,000 feet! It's really pleasant.

> September 9, 1936

Dear Mada,

I guess you must have your hands full by now. I've been told that teaching a bunch of kids can often be a nerve wracking process even at its best. My sympathies are entirely with you, but I guess after all you must enjoy it a lot.

We went to Kerrville this morning on an attack mission, completely "destroyed" the airport there, and were intercepted on the way back by the second and third elements. Boy, there are really some beautiful mountains up there. Tomorrow we're going to Brownsville, Ft. Ringgold, and Corpus Christi.

I wish I could understand you, Redhead, but I probably never will. Oh, well, someday maybe we can get to see each other and talk some more about everything. For all I know there may still be possibilities, but I hardly dare hope for them. Yes, Lady, I'm afraid we may always be a mystery to each other.

If I can find the school, I'll buzz it when we're coming back from round the Horn. Take care of yourself and write me if you care to.

Always,
C. L.

Barksdale Air Base
Shreveport, LA
January 10, 1937

Dear Mada,

Sorry for waiting so long to write, but I've been pretty much on the go lately. I was down at Brownwood Christmas Eve and then the following Monday or Tuesday, I don't remember now. I think I buzzed everyone's house within a 5-mile radius of Buffalo School, but never did see you. (I can always spot you by that flaming red hair.)

Which reminds me, my good luck lock of red hair has become faded and I'm having no end of accidents. Please, can I have another fresh one before something more serious happens to me? Put a blue ribbon on it, too.

I've been attending the First Baptist Church here in Shreveport and really enjoy the services. Dr. Dodd (he was in Brownwood one time) is the pastor and he's pretty well up on what he is talking about. They also have a well trained choir. Their best bass singer is an enlisted man here on the field and, boy, is he a "crackerjack." I didn't know before that the army was very well represented in churches, and today I saw several officers and enlisted men there. I found out long ago that the Air Corps is a far-flung contrast with the Infantry or any other arm of the service, all of which makes me feel not a little proud of being with them.

We're conducting the regular six weeks' winter test flight in Maine this February, but I don't think they're letting anyone but second-year pilots go on it. I'd sure like to go with them and see some of that forty below weather they have there. They're planning on using a frozen lake surface for the airdrome—"home on an iceberg."

At present it is raining cats and little puppy dogs outside, and has been doing so the past three days. This Louisiana weather and Mr. Scott don't get along very well, especially when it interferes with week-end cross countries.

This most humble person requests permission to be excused so he can hit the proverbial hay and knock off a bit of that proverbial "shut-eye" of which he is in dire need.

Pardon this terrible writing. That's one thing I forgot to do while in school. Wish you would tell me which place you're living in, how do I get to it from the road running in front of the school? Maybe so I can find you next time if you'll give me directions. Also describe the place, color of house, whether or not it has a windmill, if so where located in respect to house; how many trees to look for in the yard, etc. I'll try to knock the roof off when I get there (When and if).

Yours,
C. L.

Receiving letters from C. L. and settling down to the routine of teaching along with home duties filled the autumn days. Autumn had always been my favorite season. The haze over multicolored trees, the crisp air, the just-right temperature all gave me an invigorating desire to live and do for others.

C. L. did find the school and buzzed it. The superintendent rang the bell for recess, so all the school was on the playground to see him bank and turn and buzz the school again and again. Airplanes were not common then, so it was fun for all of us to see him fly over.

Yet I became restless at times. There were no social activities. I was twenty years old now and had no young people to be with. It seemed ages since I had had a date. C. L. mentioned wanting to find the house. But there was no windmill—no mark of identification—just a little unpainted house by the side of a dirt road. We had only the barest necessities.

We did have a cow and Mama tended to the milking. Daddy was sick so much, retiring early in the evening to his room. Seeing his light on later at night, I knew he was reading his Bible.

Thankful we were that I made ninety-five dollars a month. This did take care of the rent and buy our groceries. I managed to buy a used car so we could occasionally go into town.

Christmas time arrived, and Bubba and his wife came for a few days. How thrilled I was to get a beautiful manicure set from C. L. that Christmas! I really didn't expect a gift, but I cherished the fact that he gave it. And I kept in my heart the truth that the Lord gave the best Gift: "Now thanks be unto God for His unspeakable Gift." II Corinthians 9:15.

C. L. was now stationed at Barksdale Air Force Base near Shreveport, Louisiana. One day in January he found our house and came for a visit. I was not expecting him, but was so excited that he had driven out from Brownwood that weekend to see me.

CHAPTER THREE

MOONLIGHT WITH STARS

February 14, 1937

Dearest Mada,

I wanted to come over today but figured I'd better save a little bit for some other weekend. Besides, I might get on your nerves by hounding you to death.

Some guy from Alabama preached today, a Doc McGuire, who's been conducting the college revival. He sounded like an old fashioned preacher—he's O.K.

I went to dinner with Professor Winebrenner today and his illustrious son, Louis, at the dormitory. Most of the students were strangers to me.

Did I remember to tell you that I adore you, Beautiful Lady?

Love,
C. L.

On February 12 C. L. came for me. We drove to the hill overlooking Brownwood. The night was clear and starlit. The lights of Brownwood seemed to be reflections of the stars.

C. L. took me in his arms and asked me to marry him. Then our kiss sealed our promise to each other. [He later told me that he had to ask me to marry him before I would let him kiss me—which was true.] Our love was pure, love given from above to our hearts. No joy in my life exceeded my joy at this time except the joy of conversion to Christ. I felt as Elizabeth Barrett Browning did when she wrote these lines to Robert:

> "The Face of all the world has changed for me
> Since first I heard the footsteps of thy soul."

Yes, I now seemed to know C. L.'s soul—such a noble soul, so fine, so worthy. It was at that moment my soul and C. L.'s soul were entwined forever.

Sunday Night
Barksdale

Dearest,

After sitting here forty minutes trying to think of something to write, I'm still in the same fix I was at first.

I can just sit here and wish I could see you, hold you in my arms and kiss you. And then realize the futility of it all when I think of the long years ahead of us before we can form a partnership. Why in thunder were we born poor? "Hit ain't right!" But there'll come a day; you wait and see.

Okay, I won't land again up there in the oat field. I don't think you'll have to do much persuading to keep me out of that field—it's too small and not level enough. I'm sorry I scared you landing there Sunday.

You worry too much about accidents that'll never happen, though. Here's the key to the whole thing; at least, the one I use: A good physical condition, a happy mental attitude, confidence in one's ability in handling airplanes, backed by the best of training and experience, is 50 percent in winning in the flying game. The other 50 percent lies in the fact that he is able to believe himself when he gets in a tight spot and repeats: "The Lord is my Shepherd; I shall not want." Also when he hits bad weather at night and is able to feel confident when he says: "Yea, though I walk through the valley of the shadow of death, I will fear no evil, for Thou art with me."

So you see, my Darling, I can't lose; so there's no need in worrying about my ever losing. I'll tell you a story sometime about a famous airmail pilot—I believe it was Jack Knight—that will illustrate the point.

Boy, I'd sure like to come home this weekend, for it will be our last chance to get a cross-country-flight until after maneuvers on the West Coast. And my last chance to see the sweetest girl on earth, until July.

Lots of love,
C. L.

Thursday, April 20

Dearest,

The cake got here O.K. and it's really good, as will many of my "fine-feathered friends" vouch. I have it hidden away for a few days, though. The four hours you spent making it were well spent, for it was joyously received by eager hands and a hearty appetite. Thanks a million.

Incidentally, you should feel proud of yourself in the fact that one of the most important merits of woman lies in knowing how to cook. If it's all right to say so, I think you're tops, my dear, in more ways than one.

I'm moving again this evening to the Bachelor Officer's Quarters. I think this is the 14th or 15th time I've moved in the Army, and I'm about ready to settle down steady for awhile.

Well, I don't have to ride a truck or train to California. They're giving Pharr and me a couple of ships from the Third Wing. Big shots' personal ships. We call 'em the "Golden Calves," and off goes our heads if we should accidentally scratch the paint on them. So we're none too exuberant under the idea that we'll both be with our necks under the ax from the time we leave here until we get back.

Boy, I still want in Pursuit if it's the last thing I do. This morning I was in a PT-3 and had an hour dogfighting with Keith in a P-26, and he really ran me ragged. Top speed of the PT is about 80, while the P-26 has a top speed of 220. He would climb up to 8,000 ft. and make a pass at us in a long power dive making nearly 300 MPH when he came by. We could even hear his engine howling when he came by, which is a rare thing to hear from another airplane above the noise of your own engine. Man alive, but I've never seen anything go that fast before in all my life. I'd sure like to fly one of those babies and if I ever get to bring one to Brownwood, I'll really get to tear that town apart for once.

Pardon the enthusiasm over such a thing as an airplane, but I sometimes get that way. You would, too, if you could understand the thrills we sometimes get.

Thanks again for the cake. It's really swell. And so are you, my Dear.

Please, Miss Sparks, will you be my sweetheart? I'll love you always.

C. L.

P.S. I had more fun last night reading all the letters I have from you—some of them several years old, when we went together in Howard Payne College. And you signed most of them "Always yours," and I was so foolish not to think that you probably could have meant it. Oh, Mada Darling, I want to be with you forever.

Thursday Evening
April 29

Dearest,

After sleeping all evening and reading a lot of Browning's poetry, I feel pretty good and ready to take on the weather ship again tonight. Last night was really beautiful, except for some ground fog that kept trying to form. A solid canopy of fluffy clouds covered most of the lower air at about a thousand feet. They were dazzling white with the bright moonlight shining on them. I wish you could see something like that sometime. I flew until early dawn trying to reach the maximum altitude. It took two hours getting up, and only ten minutes to come down.

And today I ran across a verse that perfectly fitted this morning. (Not wanting to bore you by turning poetic, but I still like the verse) "Heah 'tis:"

> "Oh, what a dawn of day!
> How the April sun feels like May!
> All is blue again
> After last night's rain
> And the South wind dries the hawthorn-spray
> Only, my Love's away!
> I'd as lief that the blue were gray."

And I would tell you more, but I'm afraid you'll begin to take some stock in the saying that all poetic-inclined persons are just a bit "teched in the haid." Besides, I just listened to a beautiful rendition of "Ave Maria" on the radio, and now one of "Schubert's Serenade," and it might make me worse than ordinary.

So pay no attention to my blarney, Honey, and I'll come down to earth with the rest of the mortals for awhile.

I don't know all of that song you mentioned; the words, I mean. I can never remember the

Moonlight with Stars

words of a song, nor the music either until I've heard it a hundred times or so. All I know is:

"Goodnight, my Love—
The tired Old moon is descending.
Goodnight, my Love—
My moment with you soon is ending . . ."

So far as I know now, I'll probably be able to see Lake Brownwood when we start for the West Coast Tuesday. The flight line passes through Dublin and I can see the lake and Santa Anna mountain from there, if it's daylight then. We'll pass through just about dawn, I think. If I were by myself, I'd come by and buzz the school, but I'll be in a formation with 26 other airplanes. We'll leave here about 5:00 A.M. and get to Delano at dark that day, we hope.

Our address may be changed when we get there. I expect it will be. So I'll let you know the correct one as soon as I can.

Oh, my dearest golden haired lass, but it would indeed be swell to be with you tonight. The nights are getting to be ideal for a boy to court a lovely girl—no foolin'! Especially red-headed girls.

I'm glad somebody thinks my letter's interesting. I don't think they're so hot. If I read them over, I always tear them up, so you very seldom get the revised editions.

Mada, Darling, I'll love you forever, and then a thousand years after that.

                                            C. L.

P.S. Have grown a sorry, droopy moustache like bartenders wore back in the hey-day of Lilly Lantry and Queen Victoria. Am not going to cut the brush until Major Morris gets tired of looking at me and gives me a cross-country flight home soon after maneuvers.

. . . . .

Days held a touch of expectancy and warmth as I taught my first graders. Life seemed to have more zest and meaning, and I enjoyed the days with the children. I looked forward to the times C. L. could fly over.

Once when some relatives were visiting us, he landed in a plowed field by the house. Such daring! Of course there were other liberties he took with Uncle Sam's airplanes, because of his love for adventure and flying—and his desire to see me. Those days were exciting. Once he flew over my house and dropped me a note securely tied to a rock.

Another time he landed in a plowed field and asked me to fly to Brownwood with him. He would later bring me back in the car. Daddy and Mama thought that would be fine and I was so excited. We flew there in such a short time, skimming low at times just above Brownwood Lake! It was great fun!

My teaching was getting a little easier. At the first of the year I had had much trouble trying to get the subjects all taught each day. Also I had trouble keeping order as I should. I found that first graders need help in more ways than in book learning. There were hurt feelings to soothe, shoes to tie, and encouragement to be given. I was beginning to wonder if I had learned anything about how to teach while at Howard Payne College.

But somehow as spring came on the children were reading. That in itself was a miracle! They could write some and knew some numbers. They told me many things—things their parents never knew they told. Yes, six and seven year olds were a delight to be with. And to see their progress in the first grade was most rewarding.

C. L. was getting ready for manuevers on the West Coast. He was still a Flying Cadet, but a very skilled pilot. It would be some time before I could see him again. Separation was not easy for those so much in love as we were. Circumstances seemed to point toward waiting even months before we could be married—maybe years. I needed to help Daddy and Mama, and C. L. was just beginning his career. Through waiting we were learning patience, but the lessons seemed hard. Yet we must never let our longing spoil our living in the present.

Wednesday Night
May 5

Dearest,

Camp is all fixed up now so I guess I can sit down and take it easy for awhile. Pardon the pencil, but it's all I have here.

We're about a mile from Delano, a town about

twice as large as Santa Anna. Our 28 ships sure crowd this little airport, too. The weather is hot during the day and cold at night. I'm using six blankets and still got cold last night. The air from the tops of the snow-capped mountains settles in these flat valleys at night, I guess.

The mountains are beautiful and can be seen from an unbelievable distance if the air is not hazy. I could see a mountain range yesterday while we were flying over here at 8,000 feet. Most of its highest peaks were snow-covered, and it was over 200 miles away! They say you can sometimes see farther than that when the visibility is almost perfect.

We're using tomorrow for familiarization flights over the surrounding country, so Pharr, Kunze and I are going up to Sequoia National Park and see some good scenery. Then we're going over to Muroc Dry Lake where our enemy, the Pursuit, are camped and give them a good working-over.

There's a funny little bird of some sort not far from our tent, making a lonely cry sounding something like a whistling "chuck-kaw'." The desert air here gets cold and unearthly still for some reason or other. I like it because sleeping is swell. I'm completely sold on California, especially along the San Joaquin Valley. It would really be nice if we could be transferred some day to March or Hamilton Fields; this is certainly the garden of Allah or something. It would really make an ideal home.

Some of the new silver-colored A-17-A's from March flew over here today, and they really look sleek and fast. They're same as our A-17, except they're all metal, unpainted, and have wheels which retract into the body after taking off, giving less air resistance. We're due to get some of them this summer sometime.

The address is still the same, I guess—(13th Attack Sqdn. c/o Base Commander, Hamilton Field). I'm sending this letter airmail so you can answer it in time for it to get here inside of a week, maybe.

Take it easy, Darling. I love you very, very much tonight—more than ever, because you seem so far way (and I guess you are "quite a fur-piece") Write soon, because it's lonely I am for you, Dearest.

Lots of love,
C. L.

P.S. Here's the other goodnight kiss that went with the last one—X X X X X X X X X X. Say, what wouldn't I give for that to be real!

Saturday Night

Dearest Mada,

I wrote you a letter the other day, but don't know whether you'll get it or not. Our mail plane cracked up in Tejan Pass shortly after leaving here, and the letter may have been on it, although I'm not sure. The pilot, Captain Robbins, jumped and wasn't hurt so far as we know.

Tonight I have the unhappy fortune to be O.D. for Todd so he could go home. Everyone and his dog has gone into town, except for those who went to Los Angeles for the week-end. I want to go there if I can and go through Hollywood just out of pure curiosity to see a screen star once.

Did you ever hear of the famous "Death Valley Scotty," a prospector who struck the only gold in Death Valley and became fabulously rich? He lives not far from the range of mountains east of here. He built himself a million-and-a-half dollar home out in Death Valley, didn't like it, so he closed it up and now lives in a small shack at the entrance of his gold mine. I think it would be a good idea for me to tell him I'm one of his long-lost relatives and move in on the old boy!

The Attack Group had a warm-up preliminary attack on Muroc Dry Lake this morning. Eighty-four A-17 airplanes swarmed through the snow-capped mountains of Tejan Pass and proceeded to wreak havoc upon the Pursuit Airdrome in a simulated attack. I noticed all the PB-2 Pursuit ships were on the ground there. The PB's are liquid-cooled ships from Langley Field, and they're having so much trouble with their cooling systems in this hot weather, that they get very little service from them. They must be strictly a cold weather airplane, I guess.

There's a wild peacock that keeps me awake off and on during the night with his crazy scream.

Did you ever hear a peacock scream? They're very distracting, to say the least. Todd tells me that this whole valley is full of wild peafowl and they have a season to hunt them.

Do you know, my Darling, that I love you tonight same as any other night, and for all nights to come. For you're no longer the elusive, absolutely unattainable Lygian princess for whom the Roman soldier Vinituis desperately sought and fought for—but merely an adorable, realistic, honest-to-goodness girl who amazingly is not incapable of saying, "I love you" to the most surprised boy in the world—a girl for whom many a boy would passionately strive to have and to hold all his life.

Goodnight, sleep tight. Write soon.

Lots of love,
C. L.

P.S. I've acquired a taste for strawberries. You should see some of the big ones they raise here. General Brant flew over here from Bakersfield today just to get to eat some strawberries our mess officer had brought.

Monday Night,

My Darling,

Mail's pretty fair lately. I got a letter from you for 4 days straight, but one was 13 days late (the one you wrote the Sunday before I left). They're mighty fine, though.

The G.H.Q. means "General Headquarters" Air Force, in other words the air combat forces of the whole army. "O.D." is short for Officer of the Day, a temporary official who's responsible for everything from meeting a visiting General to getting rid of all stray cats and dogs.

We went to Sequoia yesterday even if I didn't get to go to L.A. or 'Frisco. We were allowed only three ships per flight for week-end X.C.'s, and cadets were outranked. Sequoia is unimaginably beautiful and awe-inspiring. It has a giant Redwood forest in which General Sherman is the largest living tree in the world. Even after you see it you can't believe it—it's so enormous. Lumberman have estimated that forty 5-room houses could be built from the lumber in that one tree. It was standing there a thousand years before Christ was born. Reminds me of a giant sentinel silently guarding the forest when the earth was young.

We had lots of fun throwing snowballs at each other and at the chipmunks. Also fed some wild deer. They're actually so tame they'll eat out of your hand.

I never hope to see a more beautiful place. Would you be interested in a honeymoon there?

Your new kittens may be cute, but they'd be much cuter if they were puppies. If you should run across a fox terrier pup, I'm in the market for one. That is, at a very reasonable price.

Todd lives only 40 miles from here so he goes

home every day. He's invited all the cadets to his home at Visalia next Wednesday for dinner, and I think we'll all accept and get a home-cooked meal once again.

The War is still on. We get up at 1:00 or 2:00 A.M. and fly over the Peashooters and their camp. Beginning in the morning we're using real tear gas. The initial load is going to be 300 gallons of the stuff. They will be crying for a week after that hits 'em.

I just finished a long letter of congratulations, etc., to my brother J. Fred who's graduating from Brownwood Hi this spring. It's a fine boy he is, as are all my brothers.

Miss Sparks, I'd give anything to take you in my arms tonight and kiss you and kiss you again and again—and again. And I'll do that very thing the next chance I get, in spite of any and all protests you may make; for you see, you're my sweetheart, and I love you.

C. L.

CHAPTER FOUR
DAYS OF WAITING

SPRING COMES DANCING

Breeze is so gentle and right
Clouds all fluffy, soft and bright
Sky's as blue as blue can be
Spring has come dancing in, you see

Crocus aflame, daffodils nod
Green blades creeping up through the sod
Tree buds ready to burst apart
Spring has come dancing into my heart.

Robins and bluebirds color the sky
Frogs a-croaking in places not dry
People whistle as they go along
"Spring has come dancing" is my song.

Boys and girls with cheeks so fair
Laughing eyes and wind-blown hair
Sadness, get behind the door!
Spring has come dancing in once more.
—Mada Scott

Yes, Spring with all its freshness, and newness was here. There were blackberries to pick, jelly to make (also blackberry pies). End of school festivities included a picnic in a nearby wooded area for the children and the teachers of Buffalo school.

When school ended, Daddy, Mama and I moved back to our farm near Comanche, which was only about fifty miles away. We had a little house there which had formerly been my playhouse when I was a child, so the renters on the farm were not disturbed by our coming. Usually we stayed outside under the trees except when we were canning fruit or gathering it in the orchard. On that hillside there was usually a breeze even on the hottest days.

The "War" on the West Coast was over and C. L. was back at Barksdale Field. I received a card from him that he would be landing in Brownwood the next week-end and would be driving over to see me (only about thirty miles).

Mama had recently made me a lime green dotted-swiss dress which I planned to wear when C. L. came.

That evening my hair had been freshly shampooed, and after bath, I dressed in my crisp green dress. I saw C. L.'s car coming up the dusty country lane, and I was outside to meet him. After greeting all, he and I drove into town. It was only when we were alone that he took me in his arms and kissed me. C. L. liked my dress so much that he wanted me to have a green wedding dress!

Life seemed so right, so comfortable with him. We had lots to talk about while we were in the Owl Drug store and while we were riding around.

We sat in the car out at the farm for a long time. In fact we were oblivious of time. Nothing seemed to matter but that we were together.

It was late when he left and my heart was disturbed, for it was raining hard, lightning and thundering. Daddy and Mama had moved our mattresses in earlier, so we must stay inside that night. I prayed for C. L.'s safety and soon drifted off to sleep.

Tuesday Night

My darling Sweetheart,

Here we are again with several hundred miles between us, and I imagine we'll be that way for quite awhile now. Now do you regret the last kiss?

It's all due to the foolish urgings of my empty head, though. I decided to go on to San Antonio and get the uniform fitted again, when I should have returned the shortest way, by Dallas; and it seems as how they didn't like it here. I got in to San Antonio rather late, too, and decided to wait and go back in the morning, and neither did that please them. I haven't seen the Major or the Colonel, but Estes and Howes assured me that the Major has definite intentions of taking away all my cross country privileges and may even ground me for a month or so. Nice, isn't it? I think I deserve a brass button for that.

About the only place I can get a ride to is San Antonio. Most of the pilots go there on the weekend; so maybe I can see you if you're there some weekend soon.

Mother made a shortcake with the berries, and it was really good. I don't remember thanking you for them, but they were certainly appreciated. Do you know how to make shortcake? If so, you may have to make lots of them in your future life.

You're probably wondering how we got off the field. I found a fairly hard ridge through the field and was taxiing out to it and got stuck in a puddle. We worked several hours and finally had to get the C.C.C. men to help get the ship out. We then took out everything we could get loose from the ship and I managed to jump the fence and get off. Then I landed at the new airport north of town (it has a hard surface runway), and picked up the passenger and baggage. I wish now I had stayed another night and hitch-hiked to Comanche and you. Mada, Darling, you've no idea how much you're being missed tonight and all other nights.

I live and think a year ahead all the time, wishing it were now that we could be together for always; but after all, it's probably best not to rush too much for there's lots to be done. But won't it be swell when we can work and plan together in one of the most wonderful institutions in the world? (I think marriage is called an institution). Anyway, it seems almost too good to be true.

Honey, if you're not the prettiest colleen that

ever breathed, there're just absolutely not any pretty girls anywhere.

We dragged the railroad station at Lexington. I didn't know where your uncle lived.

Write and tell me all the news soon as you can. Do you know whether or not you'll go to San Antonio this week? I can get a ride down Friday night with somebody, I think.

I love you, Dearest,
C. L.

P.S. The address will be "Lieutenant" instead of "Cadet," I guess. They're giving us bars tomorrow. Hot dawg, hotcha, hurray for Congress! or something.

July 9, 1937

Mada, Dear,

It's been pretty hot here today. I think it should rain tonight or tomorrow. Sultry weather, this Louisiana.

Two more pilots resigned to go to work for Braniff and Pan-American. Seems they're all leaving the Army to get along the best way it can, and I don't blame them.

I've had a gloomy, morose feeling on all day for some reason. Must be the weather, it's been pretty hot here today.

Mada, there's something I've got to say to you—something I've had on my mind for several days and I'm going to have a tough time getting it said. I'd rather take a beating every day for the rest of my life than to start telling you what I've got to.

Were you ever haunted by an unpleasant feeling until you couldn't sleep at night. Something that you knew was your fault, and yet it was something you were powerless to prevent, and knowing all the time that you'd hate yourself all the rest of your days because you'd played with the emotions of a really sincere person?

It's difficult to put in the exact words just what I want to say. I wish it were just so easy as telling another person to write it for me. I'd leave it up to some of my more learned friends here to do the job.

Do you remember my telling you one time that I was a person of great emotional instability and incurable fickleness, and we jokingly compared the heart lines in our palms, and you remarked about it?

Maybe it's the same trouble Woody Smith and Winnie D. had, I don't know. Anyway you know you said that he didn't believe in "Absence makes the heart grow fonder" and all that sort of stuff? And you'll have to admit that being away from a person so long a time sometimes causes one's feelings to grow more faint, or something to that effect. Even with no one else to divert one's feelings elsewhere, it sometimes happens that his love can entirely fade out of the picture. It often does.

We may as well quit beating around the bush, Mada, and get down to bedrock fact. I'd rather ask you something first, though, if you don't mind. And don't give me the answer I'd rather have, just because you're the same fine, splendid, true-blue girl you've always been, but really tell me the truth about it. If a hen-and-a-half lays an egg-and-a-half in a day-in-a-half, how many eggs would four hens lay in eight days? They can only lay during daylight hours. Night work doesn't count, and one of the hens lays an egg every third night, thereby making the problem more difficult.

Oh, Mada Darling, I love you with all my heart, mind, body, and soul—and sit here each night looking at your picture, wanting you madly every minute during the day, and now I've started dreaming about you each night. It seems like I haven't seen you for eternity, and time has long ago lost any meaning it might have had. Averill looks sadly in at me from his apartment and swears I've gone mad. If anyone could go mad from sheer love of a girl, then I've surely done it.

I got to fly my first transport ship yesterday, the C-14, a big Fokker cargo plane. I had eight passengers, too. (They must have been crazy or foolhardy to ride, or maybe they didn't know I'd never flown the thing before). It was almost as thrilling as the first solo at Randolph.

A pilot in the 90th Squadron landed one of the new A-17-A's today with the wheels retracted. Everyone has been expecting it to happen, but we weren't expecting it so soon. The wheels fold up into the wings after taking off, to increase the speed. They're operated electrically, and he just forgot to lower them before landing. The propellor tips and the flaps were damaged. Outside of that I guess the ship is not damaged noticeably. The A's are really nice. We have ten of them in our squadron, and I got to fly one the other day. They're much faster than the A-17, especially around 8,000 feet. They're also faster in diving. I got 310 MPH the other day in a short dive. No telling what they'd do in a test dive.

I tried to make you feel anxious in the first part of the letter, but reckon I'm not gifted in doing it the way you did one time. I think it hurt me more in writing it than it did you in reading it, anyway.

Do you know, my Dearest, that you're the prettiest, sweetest, most lovable sweetheart any boy ever had; and I love you with all the tenderness and yet all the fierceness that man can love woman. Write soon, Darling.

C. L.

Saturday
August 28
Galveston, Texas

Dearest Sweetheart,

We're here for nine days Gunnery Camp. I've the whole weekend and the whole camp to myself, and nothing to do with it. All the officers are gone on [cross-country] flights, and I still have two weeks to go yet in the doghouse.

I'm really glad you dropped in to see Mother. She had been wanting you to come see her. Was towing targets the other day and got one hung up on the bottom of the ship. The tow rope nor the target wouldn't release, so that gave an excuse to try to dive it off. I climbed up to 4,000 feet and started down, and the thing came loose quicker than I expected. It fell about a mile out in the bay, where the crash boat picked it up.

Say, you should see the Gulf from the air. You can see all kinds of deep sea animals that have come in close. There have been several giant rayfish lately, some of them as wide as the length of an automobile. They're sometimes called the "Bat of the Sea"—look like a huge black bat. They have a mouth large enough to swallow a man whole without even chewing on him. We've been practicing on them with the guns, and Lt. Morris killed one, but it hasn't washed up on the beach yet. There are also lots of porpoise, a big black fish that looks like a hog. They're really mammals, like the whale, and are very congenial old fellows. And a big deep sea turtle came in close the other day; they're supposed to be the longest-lived creatures alive today. The sea probably holds more mystery and interesting animals than any other place in the world.

Recently there have been about 12 Reserve officers who resigned their active duty to instruct in the Chinese Air Force—four of them from Barksdale. Several were here in Galveston getting ready to leave, when Uncle Sam decided he didn't like the idea, so their passports were cancelled. It may mean a step toward getting more regular commissions in the Air Corps. I hope so.

Honey, the mosquitoes here are so big we have to keep a fire axe handy to knock them in the head. About dusk they have an assembly point over my tent at 5,000 feet (four squadrons, and they sound like they're powered with the latest type Allison engines). And their beaks are equipped with diamond-tipped steel drills, electrically operated. About 9:00 o'clock you can hear them discussing what to do with you. Here's a sample of last night's mosquito talk:

"Boys, shall we eat him here or take him with us?" "We'd better take him; if we leave him here the big ones may take him away from us."

You'll be teaching school again when I next see you, I guess. What grades do you have this year, or do you know yet? Don't know for sure when I'll be home, Honey, though I hope in two weeks from today. I've quit making any kind of promise, because they could take a sudden notion to send us to Cuba or Panama or Hawaii on one hour's notice—in other words, they can send us anywhere, anytime, without telling why, and it's the way they usually do. The Army gets whims and changes of mind.

Sure, I have heart trouble—the worst kind. It

has to do with a young red-headed lady, whom I've missed so much—but from whom I've been away so long she'll seem like a perfect stranger when finally we see each other again. In case you see her, though, will you tell her I love her quite a bit here and there and everywhere—mostly everywhere at all times.

C. L.

P.S. I still think green is better than brown or black. It gives you an added look of mystery or something. Or maybe you like brown better. I'm a poor judge of clothes at any rate.

X X X X—These are kisses I've missed out on lately. I'll get even someday. I'm way behind at present.

. . . . .

Friday Night

Dearest,

I suppose you've already moved to Buffalo and are ready for school to start Monday. Time sure passes fast—sometimes I think it's only an illusion. It seems only yesterday that you were starting in your first year of teaching and I was at Kelly bucking at the harness to get home—same as I want to get home to see you now.

Raymond and I have been moving yesterday and today and still don't have everything straightened out. We moved in together in a larger room than the one I had.

Days of Waiting

I'm scheduled to go to New York week after next for a few days, but am not banking too much on it for fear it won't turn out to be true. The group is going for a demonstration during the American Legion convention. So far as I know, I'll still get to go home a week from tomorrow, I hope, I hope, I hope.

We've really been busy the past week searching for the Kelly Field Cadet who left here at night for San Antonio and hasn't been seen since. He ran into a storm near Grapeland and evidently crashed somewhere within 100 miles radius of there. We can't find any sign of his ship and doubt if they'll ever find it. Probably he crashed in a swamp along the Trinity River bottoms. Moral: Old Man Weather just can't be beaten. For the past thirty years airmen have tried to beat the weather, and it just can't be done until radio equipment has been perfected and made foolproof.

I have a copy of Elbert Hubbard's Scrap Book and am sure proud of it. A good looking book, too—bound in tan-embossed leather.

I've always wanted to own a rifle but never did—and now I've got one, a good one, too. It's a Mossberg .22 bolt action repeater with a telescope sight. Raymond and I tried it out today over at the skeet range and it's really a honey.

Autumn will be here very soon, or maybe it's already here. At least summer's nearly over, and I can smell autumn in the air. That's the season

I like best, for it has a strange, wild, exhilarating effect. If you want a thrill, just listen at dusk soon to the wild honking of Canada geese heading South, and take a good deep breath of cold, clean air that you can get only in Indian summer. It's mighty hard to beat.

Am I still in the race when I get back, or have you met some young man this summer who talks better and longer than I can and who's good-looking as all get-out? A lot of water passes under the bridge in three months, and I still maintain as how it's practically impossible to hold a gal if you're away and you have competition at home. If there's any competition, though, I'll break his neck and yours too.

Love
C. L.

P.S. I almost forgot to tell you that you're adorable.

· · · · ·

Wednesday Night

Dearest,

Scott is now officially out of the doghouse and can request a cross-country flight home this coming week end. Whether or not he'll get it is something to be seen yet, but I'm hoping for the best. If I get it, Raymond will come with me, as it will be another week yet before he can get a ship on the week end. He's been going home every weekend, though, with other pilots so he won't be so disappointed as I will if we don't get to make it.

How is school? I guess all the kids are chafing in the harness because they had to quit playing and start studying. I remember I did about that age. What used to get me, though, was having to wear shoes that hurt my feet after going barefoot all summer. Did you get to go barefoot when you were a little girl? If you didn't you've never lived.

If I do get home again, I'm afraid I won't be able to land in oat fields anymore, take up unauthorized passengers, and make all the local hops I used to do. And I guess it's just as well. Kills a lot of fun, but it's too big a chance to take.

The moon tonight reminds me that I have something especially important to whisper to you Saturday night—that I love you with all I have to love you; that you're lovely and lovable; that you're my sweetheart.

C. L.

CHAPTER FIVE

GOLDEN AUTUMN

Indian summer was here. The nights were beginning to be cool and crisp; a touch of autumn was in the air, although the trees would not be dressed in their gorgeous hues until November. Days were still hot, though, and moving back to Buffalo was on the agenda.

The summer had passed somewhat rapidly. C. L. was now a Second Lieutenant and would be dressed in his officer's uniform when I next saw him. It was thrilling to think about his rapid advancement in the Air Corps, and about how he loved life to the fullest.

The excitement and rush of school's beginning came. I would teach first grade again. The children gathered with eager sun-tanned and freckled faces to begin their first year. Mama and Daddy were settled again at the same little country house and we were grateful to the Lord for His care of us.

September 11, 1937, arrived and so did C. L. There he was so erect, so handsome, and life was more beautiful than ever. That night he slipped a yellow gold ring on my left ring finger. It had a larger diamond in the center with "wings" on either side, holding five tiny diamonds each. I was so happy that he had chosen that ring with such a meaningful design. Now all who saw it would know our pledge of love to each other. The Lord was so good to us. The world seemed to take on a golden hue like my ring.

GOLDEN

Golden sunrise o'er
a golden hill
Golden forsythia and
golden daffodils
Golden grain in an
amber fold
Golden apples in
leaves of gold
Golden sunset in
a placid west
Golden thoughts of You
bring peaceful rest.
—Mada Scott

. . . . .

September 14, 1938

Dearest,

Back here again, and I want to see you just as much as I did before I got there the other day. What is it about you, may I ask, that makes you seem so indispensable and necessary?

I'm sorry I insisted so much on a wedding next September or October, when I should have stopped to think that you have an awful lot of responsibility for a girl just teaching her second year. It's a problem we've both got to figure out—how, I don't exactly know, but there must be some answer. I'll have a lot of responsibility, too, for at least another year or two. Anyway, it's your move, and we'll get married only when you get good and ready—if it's next time I get home, or five years in the future. By then the relatives on both sides should have us fairly well stocked with wedding presents, huh? (That's the Jew in me, Honey.)

They found the cadet last night. Looks like he was flying low and ran out of gas on one tank, and the reserve failed to take when he turned it on—although nobody knows exactly what happened. Anyway, last night some civilian, either through accident or intention, set fire to the brush nearby and burned up the plane and body.

We're to leave for New York Saturday or Sunday; probably be back the following Thursday, maybe in time to get a cross country home again. I'd like to see you again with that ring on your finger. It looks swell on you.

Love,
C. L.

Darling,

Monday Night
November 15

It's really raining here tonight as if it might turn real cold before morning. I'll bet some of the nights this winter will be sure enough cold.

I'm still so dizzy and so happy about the results of last weekend cross country flight home that I feel like running out in the rain and baying at the moon. The more I think of us getting married the 1st of December the better I like the idea. It seems highly practical and the best solution yet. Mother and Dad are both glad we're getting married, too. Of course that doesn't make any difference at all except that it sure feels good to know that the parents seem to be on our side of the fence. Not all young married folks are that fortunate—they usually have a battle on hand before and after getting married.

I took the ring down to Peacock's today, so it should be ready in a week. That ring must have cost plenty, for it's very heavy, and of the highest quality gold. They're only using not quite a third of it so there will be enough left to make two or three more wedding rings from it.

Say, the Howard Payne—Simmons game is on the 3rd or 4th at Abilene. We can see it on the honeymoon. That would be great fun, if we don't run into too many of your boy friends. Guess I can bristle up and growl at them, though.

Have you been to Brownwood yet to see about your dress? I think Mother is expecting you anytime this week.

You'll never know how important and how precious to me you've suddenly become, if that were possible for you to become more important. Anyhow, you know what I'm trying to say. I love you, Honey. Write me real soon, won't you?

C. L.

. . . . .

Autumn is such a beautiful season: a panorama of color, invigorating freshness and an indescribable something in the air. C. L. and I decided to be married that fall. At first we set the date for December 1, but then changed it to Sunday, November 28—soon after Thanksgiving.

Now when C. L. came in for the week-ends we would hurry and scurry here and there making our plans. We asked a friend, Aleene Tate, to sing "Because"; that would be our only song. We chose that one since some of the words of the song were: "Because God made thee mine." C. L. then told me about the first time that he saw me on campus at Howard Payne College. It was then that he told his brother Vernon that I was the girl he was going to marry. Now it was about to come true, for God had really led us to each other.

C. L.'s mother was making my wedding dress—a royal blue chiffon velvet. Mama, Daddy and I shopped for new clothes and shoes.

Our pastor, Dr. Karl Moore, was to perform the ceremony; there would be no attendants. We would enter the sanctuary together. C. L. would be in his full dress uniform with Sam Browne belt and saber. C. L. chose the music for the organist, Mrs. Keaton. The ceremony would be at 5:00 P.M., brief and sacred.

Sunday, November 28, arrived. My bridal bouquet was of sweetheart roses and we had the altar banked with ferns. The evening beams of the sun shone through the stained glass windows of the First Baptist Church as we repeated our vows before the Lord, before friends and loved ones.

We left the church soon after the wedding, taking Daddy and Mama back home. Then in the evening twilight we drove toward Kerrville and the Bluebonnet Hotel.

The oaks were still rampant with red, gold, and rust that year and the days of our honeymoon to various parts of Texas were filled with delight. We saw deer and various other wild life. We stopped by streams and other scenic places to take snapshots. C. L. had only a week's leave and it passed so rapidly. Then it was back to teaching for me and back to Barksdale for C. L. We hoped he would be able to get a cross-country flight each weekend, as we both thought it best for me to fulfill my teaching contract, if possible.

Thursday Night

Dear Mrs. Scott:

Next time you send me a telegram and scare me to death just to ask why I didn't write, I'll wear you out with a willow switch. And making it "collect," too. I'll make you go without anything to eat for two days next time I'm home.

Seriously, I was tickled pink to hear from you, after getting over being scared for a minute. I must have a telegram complex, but I thought maybe something had happened to you.

To make sure you'll get this letter Saturday, I'll mail it at the station in town tonight. I think mail is delayed about 24 hours out here at the Post Office on the field.

Sure, I saw you in the schoolyard, but was busy with both hands and couldn't wave at that time. I didn't see the kids come out, though. Guess I'd gone on toward Waco by that time.

Incidentally, I expect to be home this Saturday. It may be late when I get there, maybe that evening late, but don't go away, for I might be there after all.

I've got lots of Christmas cards to mail out, so I'd better get busy. Bet I've got more kinfolks than anyone else this side of the Mason-Dixon line.

See you in the funny paper, my pretty red-headed fraulein, or frau, I should say.

Have gone crazy and don't remember my name.

John Doe

P.S. I remember now. I'm your husband, and I love you dearly, Lady. I hope it doesn't seem long till Christmas, Darling.

· · · ·

Christmas with its beauty and blessings came. I had only five days' vacation that year, but it was wonderful to spend them with C. L. and our other loved ones. The winter days were always brightened when C. L. could come.

One weekend in February, I went to Barksdale to be with C. L. Getting to meet several of his friends and going to church with him made the trip most worthwhile. It was getting harder to be away from him, and we both knew something must be done.

Sunday Night

Dearest,

I surely hope you are home by now so you won't be so tired for teaching tomorrow. It was really hard to see you go back for some reason or other. I don't know exactly why.

We went to church tonight, but I must have slept through the sermon, for I can't remember a bit of it.

All the bachelor officers keep telling me that I was pretty lucky to get you for a wife. (I wonder why they said that—couldn't possibly have been on account of your red hair and blue eyes.) At any rate, I'm glad I got a chance to show you off to some of these birds and let them know that we only pick winners where I come from.

There's not much to write, Honey, except I wish tonight were last night, and it would be the same

tomorrow night and always to come, for that matter.
I love you, Darling.

C. L.

> A later Sunday P.M.
> A-17-A between
> Waco and Barksdale

My Darling,

It's just about twilight now so I'd better hurry and get this written before it gets too dark to see. We're at 5,000 feet, above the clouds and the moon is gorgeous—a brand new, full moon, looks like a big silver dollar setting on top of a cloud bank. Too bad we can't be together tonight.

I really had a swell weekend, Honey. You don't know how much it means to get to be with you even a short time during the week. It gets so awfully lonely over at Shreveport without you. I'll be glad when we can be together all the time.

We're flying blind now through an overcast—can't see to write.

Just came through the top. It's beautiful. The sky's a dark purple, the clouds a brilliant sea of white snowy billows, with a soft yellow moon setting it all off in a grand style. Sometimes it seems I can almost get a glimpse of the great mystery of all creation up here, entirely separated from the earth. Anyway, it will always hold a thrill for me.

Too dark to write. I'll finish this later.
I love you,
C. L.

Shreveport, La
Got here at 7:25, better than I had expected. Raymond had just got in ahead of me from Dallas. Thank you for the valentine, Dear. I hope we'll always be sweethearts and never become "just married folks."

I forgot to thank your Mother for helping you fix the lunch—It was sure good, so tell her so, will you? Next time we go we'll go to that lake that looked so pretty—won't get thirsty there. Write soon, Dearest.

Sunday Night,
March 13

Mada, Darling,

It seems ages since I've seen you and I don't think I could weather many more weekends away from you. Today has seemed so long, and it's just the beginning of another week, too.

I didn't even hear much of what the preacher was talking about today for thinking of how nice it would be if I could have been home with you. Raymond and I spent most of the time looking at all the funny hats the women are wearing now. One girl in front of us had on one that looked exactly like a beehive. Several others looked like buckets—quite an interesting variety.

The moon tonight is beautiful, with a few white clouds hurrying across it. The wind has been blowing hard all day, typical March weather. But I think Spring is really here. All the trees are budding out, and I found a lot of wild violets in the woods this afternoon.

I was out at Flag Lake today. Started to get in a boat to go out on the water to look for mudhens, and here came a big bird dog who acted as if I were his best friend and he hadn't seen me in several years. I think he belonged to the caretaker out there, an enlisted man who lives in a cabin on a hill overlooking the lake. Anyway, he jumped in the boat and off we went. He almost turned us over several times but seemed to enjoy the ride.

It's late and I have to begin an Airdrome Officer tour tomorrow. Write soon, Dearest. I'll always love you twice as much tomorrow, if that were possible. Take care of yourself, Honey.

C. L.

Wednesday Night

My Darling,

I guess the best thing we can do is to rent an apartment at the tourist courts we were in before.

Lt. Davis has one of the nice ones (by weekly rates) and he's moving on the Post the end of next week. Maybe we can get his place. It's not too far from the Field and we won't lose any money by staying there, considering all the bills are paid and linen furnished. I'd hate to rent an apartment in town and move right out again, where they will be expecting us to stay.

Now I can hardly wait for the next two days to pass so I can come home again to see you. I'm sure now that the longer we were separated, the worse it would be. I don't believe I could stand to be separated from you much longer, Darling, especially if it were a month or six weeks at a time. I'm really glad you're going to come back with me. We'll live like married people are supposed to live for awhile at least.

I love you, Dearest. I also think you're the loveliest and finest girl in the world. I can hardly wait until I see you again.

C. L.

CHAPTER SIX

CHERRY AT NOEL

April days brought changes. Daddy had already gone to the farm near Comanche for the spring and summer. I talked with members of the school board who agreed to release me from my teaching contract so that I might go to be with C. L. It was almost certain that he would be transferred somewhere soon. So a substitute teacher was hired for the rest of the school term and I told my school children good-bye (they were so dear). Mama moved out to the farm with Daddy.

I packed my "belongings" and was ready when C. L. came for me in our new shiny black Ford. It was a gay time, yet a touch of sadness, as now Mama and Daddy would be at the farm with no certain income. Bubba was in Coleman, though, and not far away. He would help.

We did find an apartment when we got to Shreveport, where we lived until June. It was evident that our first baby was on the way and we both began planning and thinking of names.

C. L. got his orders to go to Hamilton Field, near San Francisco, California. The Army would move what possessions we had, but we did take some few needed items with us in the car.

Before heading toward the Rockies, we went by Comanche, Brownwood and Coleman. C. L.

agreed that I should deposit the money I had in my bank account into Daddy's and Mama's account in Comanche, which I did. They were so grateful as they were ready to withdraw the last bit of money they had.

After telling our folks good-bye, we began the trip West. The scenery was breathtakingly beautiful, and C. L. even took me to the top of Pike's Peak in our little Ford!

We settled in a Spanish-style cottage in San Rafael, California. It was while we were there that President Roosevelt drove through the streets of that quiet town with his dog, Falla, and we waved to him as he slowly passed along a street near our house.

In Petaluma we found a less expensive house, so were there for awhile. The church we attended was very friendly and we enjoyed singing in the choir. The ladies gave me a baby shower of so many useful items, mostly blue. C. L. was due to be selected as a deacon when we decided to move again. This time it was out in the country to an area called Indian Valley. Here we had a new house and would have enough room for our little baby.

It was now late fall and the baby was due in January. We selected the name "Churchill Jackson" if a boy and "Cherry Katheryn" if a girl. Letterman General Hospital in San Francisco was the army hospital where the baby would be delivered. Riding into the city for periodic health checks was refreshing. The brisk ocean breeze, especially over the Golden Gate bridge was exhilarating. It was only a thirty-mile trip, so the doctor said we could get there in plenty of time when the delivery was due.

A short while before Christmas Mama and C. L.'s Mother came; C. L. and I had never been away from our folks for more than three months, and now we had been away for over six months. They both planned to stay for awhile to help us with the baby.

Christmas Eve was on Saturday that year. That day Mama went with me on my usual walk. Out in the country was a quiet enjoyable place to stroll, but this time when my back began to hurt, Mama suggested that we go back home. We decided to have our Christmas tree with presents that evening and it was well that we did, for on Christmas Day a short time before noon I knew it was time to go to the hospital. After putting in my bag, C. L. and I raced toward Letterman Hospital. Our little Ford seemed to have wings in the sea breeze.

Our January baby arrived as a late Christmas gift amidst the fog horn sounds in the Pacific Ocean. Cherry Katheryn, our little red-headed, blue-eyed darling, was born in the early morning of December 26. We stayed ten days in the hospital where we had excellent care.

Mama and C. L.'s Mother did all the work for several days, so when they left, C. L. and I hardly knew what to do. We felt a bit fearful with the

CHERRY AT NOEL

responsibility all ours. But how thankful we were for our precious baby! We took many kodak pictures, taking trips through wooded areas of eucalyptus trees and redwoods. We also had an overnight retreat at Yosemite National Park with its snow-capped peaks, waterfalls, bears and deer.

Taking our month's leave of absence, we drove to Texas late in April. All the folks were elated to see our little jewel. Daddy was very sick and coughed so much. He did get to see Cherry Katheryn, but he thought it best for her that he not be near her much. When I stayed with him, C. L. kept the baby in Brownwood.

Daddy and Mama were living with Bubba and his wife now. Mama took care of Daddy, taking him his meals, giving him medicine, trying to make him comfortable. When we left to return to California, Daddy told me as he embraced me that he would see me again someday, somewhere.

On June 8 we received a call that Daddy had gone to be with the Lord. Tearfully I packed a few things, and the baby and I boarded a train for Texas.

June 9, 1939

Dearest,

I've been busy all morning—had to go out to the field, but at last have three days off, so I'm going to go fishing and hang out on the creek a couple of days. This empty house gets on my nerves everytime I go in it. You've no idea how much difference it makes with you and the baby being gone.

I suppose you're well out of California by the time I'm writing this. I surely hope you manage the baby's milk and everything without getting upset. I know how you feel about that and wish we could have gone back in the car together, but there was no choice.

I inquired about being relieved from active duty. It seems that they won't pay me anything if I get relieved in the middle of the month, so I'll have to wait until the 30th. I have already sent a radiogram request and should get it confirmed in a few days, but it won't become official until the 30th. In other words, I can't get paid until the 30th.

I requested a cross-country home and should get there around the 16th or 17th (provided they approve it). Then I'll still have plenty of time to get straightened out before the 30th.

I wish I could be at the services for your Dad, but guess he'll understand that I couldn't possibly make it, and I believe he does know about it. I'm so glad he's going to be put away at Giddings, for he wanted to go back there so much. I feel somehow that he appreciates that, too. But I'm most glad that he's been relieved from all his suffering and has reached the only perfect and supreme goal that Man ever attains—that of being with Christ our Saviour.

Take care of yourself, Darling, and I'll see you soon. Kiss the Baby for me and tell her that Daddy would sure like to see her.
All the love in the world,
C. L.

> The soul
> Of God's dear saint
> Who leaves this earthbound life
> Has outgrown his dwelling for
> Freedom
> —Mada Scott

We laid Daddy's body to rest in the family plot of the cemetery in Giddings, Texas, the little town where he was born. Our hearts were grieved, but we knew he was with our Lord and Saviour, Jesus Christ.

By his own request, C. L. was dismissed from the Air Corps in the summer of 1939. He wanted to try the airlines, so we were in Tulsa, Oklahoma, for a short time. But he soon knew he had made a mistake—he wanted to be back in the Air Corps.

Mama had moved to Howard Payne College campus and was studying for a degree so that she could be back into teaching again.

In September, 1939, we were back in the Air Corps and on our way to Sacramento Air Depot where C. L. would fly transport planes carrying cargo to and from various air bases in the nation.

It was here that we so enjoyed the early learning months of Cherry Katheryn: her walking, talking, singing, playing. We took home movies and kodak pictures of her in the snow once sitting on her toboggan sled that C. L. made for her; another time in the spring, we took pictures of her in a field of orange California poppies—her golden curls glowing and blowing in the wind. The days were happy contented days. C. L. was sometimes gone for two or three days or more at a time on flights. Our dog, Fritsy, often flew with him on trips when C. L. was away. During those times the baby and I visited friends on the Base. Often an older lady or some officer's wife and baby would spend the nights with us when C. L. was not home.

Lake Tahoe was a favorite resort for us when we wanted to get away briefly. C. L. had bought us a new red Nash; he drove it from the factory which was more economical. So our months at Sacramento were most enjoyable except for the fact that C. L. had to be away from us periodically.

Friday Night

Darling,

"Another day, another dollar; a million days, a millionaire."—so goes it. But I'm tired of being away from you and the Baby. I'm afraid I'd never make a good traveling salesman.

I hope you have someone staying with you tonight so it won't be quite so lonesome. It seems terribly lonesome to me without you and the Baby.

Well, we're in the city of the Mormons once more. This place is interesting to me—it has the ancient atmosphere of early Mormon pioneering days. We're staying right across the street from Temple Square. Remember the day we went to the organ recital, when you were so sick at your stomach, and when we got back out our dog Fritzy was about to burn up in the car?

Remember when we came across Nevada how many mosquitoes there were? Through Winnemucca, Battle Mountain, Lovelock, Reno. I saw all of them again today on the way into Salt Lake.

Don't know how far we'll get tomorrow. First stop will probably be North Platte, Nebraska, then maybe on into Chanute Field, Illinois. Then maybe Sunday we can get back into Langley and start back. Looks like it will be Tuesday before we get back to Sacramento. Wish we were going back tonight.

Beggars can't be choosers, though, or something similar.

I love you both, Darlings. A thousand kisses for you.

C. L.

Somewhere in Iowa
Thursday (I think)

Darling,
I've been trying to get a letter off to you all

day, but somehow haven't been able to make it until now, and it's getting dark so I'll have to get it "writ" in a hurry.

The new car is a beauty, and really nice driving. Haven't had a chance to use the bed yet, altho I caught a couple hours sleep last night in the back seat. Had to take the train up to Kenosha from Chanute. Didn't get in Kenosha until 8:30 P.M., and the factory was closed, but I had phoned them from Chanute and they left the car with a Nash dealer in town. It was sure hard to have to poke along at 25 mph for 250 miles—then 35 for another 250. But its getting enough mileage so I can drive about 45 and make more time.

Sure wish I had you and the little girl with me, but we'd have to have more leave. This is really going to be a grind if I get in on schedule. I've got to get some sleep tonight, though, as Fritzy and I are both "pooped."

Hon, I sent $50 to the bank, so maybe you'd better enter it on our check book.

I'm sure tickled over the new car and glad we got it now instead of waiting till the price went up. It's really flashy looking.

Got to hit the road and find a place to camp. A million kisses to my sweetheart—and the same number to my little sweetheart.

All my love,
C. L.

C. L. in 1943

Mada in 1943

(*Top left*) C. L. when in college (1935).
(*Top right*) C. L. in 1936. (*Bottom right*)
C. L. and Cherry near Lake Tahoe,
California (1940).

(*Top left*) C. L. and April (San Antonio, Texas, 1942). (*Top right*) C. L. and Madell on our farm near Brownwood, Texas (1943). (*Bottom left*) Cherry, C. L., with Madell on his knee, Mada holding April (May, 1943).

CHAPTER SEVEN
APRIL IN AUGUST

In 1940 we were transferred to Kelly Field in San Antonio, Texas. Also in September, 1940, C. L. attained the rank of First Lieutenant.

We enjoyed getting to build our own house here. It was fun to select the colors and to arrange each room just as we wanted it. Several of our folks visited us often.

In 1941 we were sent to Barksdale Field, Louisiana, again. C. L. was now a Captain in the Air Force. Our second little one was due, so we chose "April Allene" if a girl, and kept the same name for a boy.

We were thrilled and excited that this time C. L. was allowed to be present at Barksdale Base Hospital when our little baby doll, April Allene, was born. She had long dark brown hair and blue eyes shielded with long lashes. She was born August 2, so Mama was able to come stay awhile to help me. She was now teaching each school year. Cherry K. was so excited about April and loved her dearly, too.

Just a month after April was born, we were ordered back to Kelly Field in San Antonio, returning to our little house we owned. It was a delight to care for the girls and to be settled awhile in our home.

December 7, 1941—Pearl Harbor Day—left us with uneasiness that C. L. might be sent overseas. But no orders came at that time.

In the Spring the Texas wildflowers were rampant. We took pictures of our little Louisiana Southern Belle nestled among the bluebonnets and Indian paintbrushes. Movies and snapshots of both Cherry and April together in colorful settings would be tokens of treasured memories in days to come. Both girls were precious gifts to us and such joys.

C. L., now a Major, was sent to Sebring, Florida, for a war training school in the summer of 1942. We decided that the girls and I should stay at Carthage, Texas, near an uncle and aunt of mine. C. L. rented a little cottage for us next door to the landlords—a fine Christian couple. I was expecting our third child in February, so C. L. made arrangements with a doctor in town for me to have periodic checks.

Sunday, August 9

My Dearest,

I'm still carrying a postcard around that I wrote yesterday. Can't get any stamps to send a letter airmail. Guess I'll get this off tomorrow anyway. Think I'd better send you a wire to let you know I'm O.K. (Hope it doesn't scare you.)

Have been plenty busy today filling out personnel questionnaires, also trying to satisfy the Finance officer with supporting papers for July pay.

I'm short some old (1939) active duty orders, so wired Kelly Field for them if they have them. Believe I can get travel pay O.K.

Glad that I've got plenty to do here. I'd go nutty wishing for you and the girls—may anyway. Here's a kiss for all of you X X X X X. Wish I could send it in person.

Rode over on the train with a Col. Brice, Judge Advocate General for the Third Air Force. He says combat crews sent to them from Sebring from now on will be given twelve weeks Operational Training before being sent to fronts. That means I'll be flying all over the U.S. and will probably get several chances to see you. Hot Dawg! Don't know how long I'll stay here—probably the full thirty days as we're having to wait for the previous class to finish.

This place is fairly well disorganized as far as training is concerned, according to everyone I've talked with. Nearly all the instructors are relatively inexperienced which increases the difficulties. Most of them have at the most one and one-half years' service, which is probably why the student pilots are so disgusted with the course.

I'm sure I'll enjoy the course, even at that, because there's plenty of studying I want to do and am glad to get the opportunity.

We all live in wooden barracks, four cots to a room, rather crowded, no desk to write on, and barracks are plenty hot day and night. Several hundred officers are in each class, so they have a housing problem here. What we have is adequate, though, and will be remembered as luxurious later in the field. I personally find life more simple this way, and even get a kick out of it. Last night I borrowed some nails and hammer from a supply sergeant and took pride in completely furnishing our room with hooks for everything. It's now all on the walls instead of the floor.

Humidity is high. Every evening it's supposed to rain and cool off somewhat. I doubt if hot weather will be so bad from now on, as the hurricane season begins this month and lasts through September and October.

It's just as well you and the girls didn't try to come with me, because of the acute housing situation.

I went to church services this morning on my rounds about the Post. Didn't last long, but I enjoyed it. They have a pipe organ, good organist, very small choir (only three today).

I hope you are keeping your mind occupied (I know you'll have plenty to keep your hands occupied). I don't want you worrying about me anymore than you want me to worry about your welfare. (I do want you to get a dog, though) I can't help thinking about you every minute during the day, but will try to think that you're playing with the girls and loving them for me, or going to the show, or buying them drinks at the drugstore (Cherry K. really likes that), or driving up to Beckville—anything instead of mooning over my absence. And I want you to think I'm spending every minute of my time training myself to the highest degree possible.

I couldn't ask for, or can't imagine a better wife than I have, Darling. You were swell—superb—even up to the time the train left, while I was just about to bust out. One tear from you and I would have boo-hooed then and there, and that would have thrown the babies into hysteria from fear of something they can't comprehend. You make me feel proud of you and honored to be your husband because you have more courage than I have, Sweetheart.

I wouldn't take the world for my wedding ring and wish now I'd let you get me one before. I'm very proud of it and all it represents. Each time I look at it I see you and our babies and our future babies, and thank God for giving you to me.

I know I have a letter from you now in the Post Office, but it's closed. Sure wish I could get it. I'll write the girls a special letter on the back.

All my love to the sweetest woman in the world,
C. L.

Thursday Night

My Darling Wife and Baby Girls,

I just got back from Palm Beach tonight too late to get the mail. I'm sure there's a letter from you, but I'll have to wait 'til morning.

We haven't done anything since the first day—

still waiting on the last class to graduate. There's nothing of interest in Sebring and certainly not here at the field, so I developed a severe case of the "crut." Finally decided to see the sights at Palm Beach, so hopped a bus over there (about 2½ hours) yesterday evening and came back today. I feel 100 percent better for some reason or other, and since we start class tomorrow I assume we'll be too busy to mope from now on out.

Palm Beach is really a beautiful place and I hope someday we can be stationed there. The beach is smooth snow-white sand sloping gradually to the ocean floor, with water crystal clear. It's quite easy to see fifty feet down under when the water's fairly smooth. I went swimming today; then fished from the pier. The pier manager showed me how, and I caught eight goggle-eyes in an hour. He cleaned some of them and served them to me for dinner in the pier grill (a small, open dining room looking out to sea). I'd have given anything if you and the girls had been there. Cherry K. and April would have had more fun playing on the beach, also looking at the fish. I saw all kinds of tropical fish (like they have in the aquarium at San Francisco) from the pier. In places the ocean floor was black with large schools of goggle-eye. I walked back to West Palm Beach to the hotel, about three miles, and detoured through some private palm groves that looked like a tropical jungle. The ground is littered with coconuts that fall off the palms. Everywhere are different-colored chameleons (look like small lizards). Most numerous were little ones about two inches long, colored a dark purple. There's not much to see at night, since they have dim-out every night. I had supper with two lieutenants from Morrison Field. We drove back to the hotel in the dark—sure is a weird feeling; makes the town look deserted. There's nothing to do or see, so I went to bed early.

According to the bulletin board I've been assigned to a crew. My co-pilot is 2nd Lieutenant South (I haven't seen him yet. Don't know who the Navigator or bombardier are). I'll report to my instructor in the morning—ahem! I think he's one of the cadets I instructed last year at Barksdale.

There's no getting around it. At times the loneliness and longing for you and the babies settles like a blanket over my head. There's only one way I can shake it off, and that's by reading from the Bible and praying. I still long for you, but the loneliness goes away then. It's amazing what restorative powers there are in faith, and I've never before realized it so much as I do now. I feel so sorry for a man who has no faith in the Divine and who feels no personal relationship with God; and there's nothing to pull him out of the depths of despair except a bottle of liquor.

I'll finish this tomorrow. It's late and I have to get up real early tomorrow; also my roommates do and I'm afraid I'm keeping them awake.
                    Goodnight, Darlings,
                    C. L.

                         Thursday, August 21
My Darling,
   I thought at first I wouldn't send you this clipping about Marion Pharr because it would make you feel bad, but I'd have to tell you sometime anyway. I wrote Mary on August 17 (same date of clipping) to find out where Marion was as I wanted to try to see him if I should be sent out where he was based. I sent the letter to Gainsville and his uncle opened it—then forwarded it to her. He wrote me and enclosed the clipping. Poor Mary—she must be nearly crazy, not knowing for sure what happened. I've got to write her and explain the possibilities of the situation, as she's undoubtedly grasping for any possible hope, of which there's quite a bit. I'm praying for his safety and I know you are, too. I don't know what kind of mission he was on, but there are favorable odds that he was forced down at sea, and even if he were hit by shellfire, the odds are still in his favor. He has two large lifecrafts and provisions, and there have been several instances of plane crews being at sea on rafts for as long as two months. If their provisions run out, they can catch rainwater for drinking. Pharr's been missing only a short

time, and there's an even chance he may show up later.

Marion was pretty much of a fatalist when we lived together at Barksdale. Whether he's changed or not, I don't know. He figured that he was either lucky or unlucky. I'm not brave enough to face the future anyday with a philosophy like that; I must ask God for protection. While I also feel that a person is destined to either leave the world at an early age or an older age, I believe that the Lord can be persuaded to change His mind and set a later date—provided that person has the faith and prays it in the Name of Christ. "Thy will be done" should not be construed as a passive acceptance of the unquestionable, unfathomable, unchangeable decision of the Almighty. I fail to see it in that light. I can't help but believe that God would bring an individual out safely from any hopeless situation provided He were convinced that the person would prove of later value in the building of His kingdom on Earth; not simply because of gratitude for saving his skin, but that he recognized the all-important, indisputable value of faith which we so often forget. We're no better, if as good, as Jesus' disciples were, when they constantly were losing sight of their faith in Him, even though He actually performed miracles before them for their benefit. Look what He did for Daniel, Moses, Jonah (whom you wouldn't have considered worth going to all that trouble for), the Hebrew children—

others—all brought through an impossible situation simply because of their faith, or because He saw a means of teaching them faith.

I know of a practical, first hand example. Your Uncle Horace told me that during World War I, he came so close to death on so many occasions that he made up his mind to accept the fact that he'd never come out alive. Then he told me that he was not converted until he was over thirty years old. Who would have thought God would go to that much trouble to save the hide of one unbeliever? It was simply that He had use for him as a leader and teacher of His Word in a little country church at Beckville—I believe that strongly.

I don't want to appear to be "whistling to keep from running," for the longest and loudest prayers in the world are of no use without faith. I simply feel that I can go through this war and any others to come, provided I ask it of Him and believe in Him and believe He will do it.

In connection with praying, I'm beginning to find out that a frantic plea is no prayer, although I've done it many times to no avail. It becomes necessary to calm oneself and easily think it out with God, pointing out the reasons why the prayer should be granted, which of course must be because Jesus would want it that way—"For Christ's sake I ask."

I remember one vivid demonstration to me of the power of prayer, and I'm ashamed that I've never told it to anyone except you now, because of its very personal nature. When I was a kid of about twelve, I think, I overheard Dad talking to Aunt Edna. He had had several financial difficulties, big hospital bills and doctor fees, and had lost faith in several preachers he'd been trying to listen to. On top of that, I think it must have been during the early days of the Depression. At any rate, I heard him say to Aunt Edna that he had lost faith in God, or words to that effect. When he said that, my world came to an end, for I seemed to recall that a statement like that was the unforgivable sin. I became panic-stricken and ran down to the creek back of Cunningham's. It was already late at night, but I felt I couldn't go back home, so I started praying. I prayed as best I knew how, which wasn't sufficient, for several hours. It wasn't until early in the morning that I began to pray logically and coherently, and after a short while, I felt that my prayer had been heard. I slipped back home, into bed, with a feeling of peace and security. Shortly after that I had the satisfaction of discovering that Dad had a renewed faith. Whether it was my prayer or Aunt Edna's (I'm sure she must have prayed) or both, I don't know. I do know that I felt afterwards that I could ask anything in His (Christ's) Name, believing, and I'd get it in direct proportion to the faith with which I had asked.

I have a simple formula that I refer to now when I read of people I knew well being "shot down in combat," "missing in action," etc., and I get an uncomfortable feeling that I might have to later fill their place in combat against the Jap or the Nazi. It's a Psalm I memorized when a kid, and received a dime from the preacher as inducement (I wonder if he knew at the time the value that dime was later). To me it is the most beautiful piece of poetry in the Bible, the 23rd Psalm, and its beauty grows. "The Lord is my shepherd, I shall not want . . . He restoreth my soul . . . yea, though I walk through the valley of the shadow of Death, I will fear no evil, for Thou art with me; Thy rod and Thy staff they comfort me . . . Surely goodness and mercy shall follow me all the days of my life, and I will dwell in the house of the Lord forever." Simple, isn't it? Then there's the one that embodies the fathomless power of Christ's promise: "Whatsoever shall ye ask in Me, believing, that shall ye also receive." It's a combination that can't be beat by any power, even the Devil himself.

Why am I telling you all this? Because I think it may help your faith in my coming through this war O.K. if I should have to go to combat which I undoubtedly will sooner or later. What prompted me to write this now was the news about Pharr. I think you can pray for his safety as I am, and it might help bring him back to Mary.

We went on sub-patrol over the sea today. Didn't see any, but had a good dose of depth charges along just in case. They're awfully hard to spot, especially when the seas are choppy and running.

The B-17 isn't as fast as I thought, but her

power turrets will reach out and knock down zeros all day long before they can get within range to fire. I put lots of faith in her abilities.

We have an early mission tomorrow—altitude flight, I think, so I'd better sign off. All my love to you the the girls.

C. L.

Friday, September 11

Darling,

We definitely are scheduled to graduate Monday, so I'll probably get to see you about the time I wrote you I would.

I'm sure I'm O.K. for private conveyance out of here, and I still plan on going to Meridian with Captain Schooling. I still believe our first stop will be to the Second Air Force at Salt Lake. We may be there only a few hours, and then out to Boise, Tucson, Seattle, or some place on the West Coast.

I missed getting sent out of here to parts unknown, within 24 hours the other day just because I knew the Training Sqdn. Commanding Officer and the Director of Training at Barksdale last summer. I'll probably have to go later on, but I want to get some operational training first—and I've also got to be with the sweetest wife and babies on earth a while longer. The war will have to wait (I'm sure it will). Seriously though, I'm wondering if I'm physically qualified for combat duty, having a stigmatism in both eyes. I'll have to pass a rigid physical exam before leaving.

Am still attending lectures in ground school. Some of them are very interesting.

Daddy enjoyed your letters, Cherry and April. He'll sure be glad to see you next week.

All my love,
C. L.

CHAPTER EIGHT

DIMPLES IN FEBRUARY

Excitement was in the September air as C. L. came in from Sebring, Florida. Tears of joy were shed; we packed our car, and were on the way to Salt Lake City. A few days there revealed we would be at Davis Monthan Air Force Base, Tucson, Arizona.

To relax we occasionally would drive out among the saquaro cacti near Tucson, finding a suitable place to enjoy a picnic.

C. L. was very busy here, often leaving for the base at 5:00 or 6:00 A.M. During the days, the girls and I enjoyed the ample room we had in the attractive house which we were leasing. It was in Tucson, near the University. In the spacious backyard, April learned to walk.

Soon after Christmas C. L. was ordered to train pilots and check crews at various air bases, so the girls and I, in a comfortable train compartment, departed for Texas since it would only be about a month until the baby came.

Sunday Night

Dearest Girls,

I'll scratch a line before I go over to the Tower tonight. I've moved into the Visiting Officers Quarters. I stayed at the house most of the afternoon, packing and cleaning. Still haven't finished everything. I'll go back tomorrow if I can stand the sight of it being empty. It seemed to me all day that you should have been there, and I kept listening for April and Cherry. I'm glad I've moved out here. If I lived to be a thousand years old, I could never get used to being away from you and the babies.

I may send another box or two by express. There's quite a lot to load into the car. I'm sending a sack of pecans I got today. They looked good and fresh.

How did April and Cherry take to the train ride? Also how do you feel after the trip? Hope you're O.K. and also hope Dad met you in Abilene on time and that you didn't have any trouble at the station with all that luggage.

I miss you so awfully much but am going to stay busy so I won't keep my mind moping about it. Hope you keep busy enough so you don't worry about me.

Kiss our darlings for me. I love you all more than I can tell you. Goodnight, Sweetheart.

            C. L.

January 1, 1943

Dearest Sweetheart,

I didn't get a letter today. Post Office was closed. Hope I get two tomorrow.

Funny thing. I've been reading this evening to break the monotony of being away from you and the girls, and of all the things I found that pulled me out of the dumps it was "Winken, Blinken, and Nod." Tell Cherry and April that we'll memorize that together the first chance we get.

I'd like for you to put my letter in the church there first time you go, if you go anymore before the baby comes. I think it would be nice if we could have our letters there together in the church—makes us seem closer together, somehow.

Have you moved into Aunt Edna's apartment yet? You'll probably be needing some of the things I have packed in the car, but it may be awhile before I can get them to you. I've decided to try to get three days off after I get to Alamogordo and drive the car home myself—then I'll get to see you. In that case it may be the middle of this month, if I can get the leave at all.

Give all our kinfolks my regards. I would write them, but don't have much time.

How's everything at the farm? I wish I could see our place, with you and the girls there now. (I mean I wish we could spend a week together there.) I love you so much, Dearest. I'm sure glad Cherry Katheryn picked you out, as she says.

All my love,
C. L.

Monday Night

Dearest Sweetheart and Girls,

Just a line to let you know I'm at Alamogordo. I flew over yesterday, flew back, and left Tucson last night. Drove halfway, stopped at Lordsburg, then came on in this morning. No flat tires, thank goodness.

This place is sure scattered out. Mess hall is one mile from my quarters. The squadrons are three to six miles apart. If I can ever get to El Paso, I'm going to look for a bicycle. I could undoubtedly sell one for a profit when I leave here.

Half my crews are still in Tucson, held up because of weather. They should have moved us by rail.

Am in a room with three other officers. It's plenty cold here inside and out. Food is pretty good so far. It's just the distance and dust that makes this place so unattractive (also tar paper buildings).

Write me at Hq. 330th, Bomb Group, A.A.B., Alamogordo. How are you feeling, Darling? Hope you're O.K. from the trip.

I've got to get some sleep. The hospital met me with needles today and I immediately got a typhus and tetanus in the same arm. The typhus sure made me sick for about an hour. That's what makes the Army so attractive, though—the Man with the Needle.

Kiss the girls for me. I love you, Sweetheart.
C. L.

January 20, 1943

My Darling Wife,

I got two letters from you today. I knew I'd hit the jackpot on mail in a day or so. I really was glad to hear from you and the girls.

Am going over to Tucson in the morning to exchange a B-24. Am taking two pilots along to check them on instrument flying. I still can't figure how I'm going to be able to check 37 crews this month. Have been holding meetings all day today—the crews get lax in their efforts unless someone keeps after them continually. Some of them are excellent, though.

Your letter is full of flattery, Dearest. I'm not worth it, but thanks just the same. I feel the same way about you, and love you more every day. I miss you an awful lot, but it's just as well you're not here, because I couldn't be with you as much as I'd want to be. This job is taking more time than I realized. I have less time off than I had at Tucson, believe it or not. And accidents still happen. I can't get away from the knowledge that I'm largely responsible for their training, but I'm going to check every pilot personally on instrument flying until I'm positive they can take care of themselves. Our next month at Topeka will give them a good chance to do actual instrument flying in an overcast, then they'll be on their own from then on—flying over new, unmapped territory without any airways as they have in the country.

I sure hope I can be with you when the baby comes. Maybe some way it can be made possible, although I don't see any at present.

I'll answer the little girls' letters, then get some sleep. Goodnight, Darling. I love you.

C. L.

Dearest Little Sweethearts,

Daddy is surely glad every time he gets a letter from you both. Cherry Katheryn, you write pretty good now. You'll have to teach April how to write like that—although she does well, too, for only one and one-half years old.

Do you girls enjoy going to Sunday School there at Brownwood? I'll bet all the other kids are glad for you to be in their class.

Daddy certainly misses you precious darlings. Give mother twice as many hugs and kisses for Daddy. I love you.

Daddy

Wednesday Night

My Darling,

I didn't get a letter from you today and am wondering if you had to go to the hospital. Still haven't received a wire, either. I hope you don't have to go for a day or so yet, because I think I may be able to get a ship and come be with you, after I get to Clovis. I went over there today (in the A-20—that's some airplane). I averaged better than 300 mph ground speed from the time of take-off to the time of landing; which meant that I was doing almost 350 half the way over. It's really fast after being around BC-1's for the past year or so.

Herblin's crews have already been moved to Clovis. I'm still giving mine instrument checks, but expect to move over tomorrow evening and have all my crews over there by Friday.

I'm coming to see you first chance I get. For some reason I'm not worried about you this time. Guess it's just because I know you'll be O.K.

Have to give some more instrument checks tomorrow and must get the required 6 hours of sleep. I love you, Dearest. I get the same thrill each time I look at your picture, as I did the first time I saw you. (My heart melts down and I get weak in the knees. I'm sure you know what I'm trying to say.) You're my sweetheart forever and sometimes I can't make myself realize it. Then when I think of our two sweet baby girls I must apologize to the Lord for not being worth my keep.

Goodnight, my Sweetheart. I'll write you again tomorrow night if I'm settled by then. Love and kisses to our precious girls.

C. L.

In Brownwood C. L.'s Aunt Edna had an apartment available, where Cherry, April, and I lived, awaiting the baby's arrival. C. L.'s mother and dad lived out on our farm which was a short distance from town, so the girls and I enjoyed visiting them occasionally during those winter days. Making preparations for the baby kept me busy, also.

Our little blond, blue-eyed baby with a dimpled cheek was born February 7, 1943, in Memorial Hospital in Brownwood, Texas. We named her "Sylvia Madell." Madell was a combination of my name, "Mada," and part of C. L.'s name. C. L. did get to come stay a few days. It was during those days that he became very dissatisfied with the care given the baby by some nurses in the hospital. So he made arrangements before he left for us to have private nurse care in our apartment. Madell was then five days old. How rich we were to have three precious daughters!

C. L. wrote this to his brother Fred after Madell was born:

"You ought to see our new girl. She's a little honey, and we weren't a bit disappointed. As a matter of fact, I rather wanted the baby to be another girl. She's fat as a butterball and is perfectly formed—has dimples in her cheeks and chin, and is red-headed as usual. Hope you can get off before long and see her."

It was a luxury to rest so much with three weeks of special care, but I was thankful C. L. had arranged it that way. Cherry and April were at the farm much of that time, thoroughly enjoying the animals and the open spaces.

Saturday P.M.

My Dearest Wife and three Baby Girls,

After a Sinbad-the-Sailor episode, I finally got here this afternoon. It's a long story.

I wonder if you're out of the hospital now. I didn't have time to go back to see you, but Miss Knight (the nurse I tried to get at first) came over to the house just as I was leaving and said she could take the case for a week or maybe two weeks (guess they told you all about it). Anyway I hired her on the spot and told Mother and Aunt Edna to get ready to move you from the hospital. (Hope you enjoyed the ambulance ride.) I think you'll be better satisfied and can get better attention at home and maybe can get as much rest if Mother can keep the girls at the farm awhile.

The car began knocking pretty badly between Coleman and Abilene, and by the time I got to Abilene it wasn't percolating very well. After a couple of hours waiting for the garage men to render a verdict after dissecting the car's innards, it was found that she would go no more until an entire new crankshaft assembly and bearings had been replaced (to the tune of approximately $135). The garage people had to have a definite decision then as they had no room on the floor for it for a couple of weeks. So I quickly made the necessary arrangements, bade the decrepit DeSoto farewell, and rushed to the bus station just in time to catch the 35 mph Special to Midland—got in there about 10:30—found out the C-78 couldn't get in there because of dust. Set out to Odessa with Irvine [C. L.'s brother] to spend the night. Left the house about 10:00 this morning.

Latest rumors are that we'll leave here as originally scheduled. Suits me—the dust is terrific.

You've no idea how much I enjoyed being with you, Dearest, and getting to be with our newest little beauty. Seems like a beautiful dream. I think I'll be able to do more work now. I wasn't in the mood to work while I was waiting for you to go to the hospital.

Played the cornet a few minutes this afternoon. I enjoyed it and think I'll keep it with me awhile. Funny thing, but I never seem to get rusty on technique—my lip muscles just poop out quickly is the main trouble. I think I'd be able to go back to playing with a band with a little lip-toughening. Someday we'll all have an orchestra—you and I and our girls.

Give Cherry, April, and Madell their Daddy's love, and a big hug and kiss for them each. I love you, my Darling.

C. L.

Sunday, February 4

My Dearest,

I sent you a wire today after I found out that there would be no mail pick-up service until Monday. I had already written you a letter last night. I thought it would go last night, but it didn't.

I've been practising on the cornet this afternoon. I sure enjoy it, and I should have it all the time. Music is a great outlet for a person's feelings, and it's surprising what effect it can have. I'm looking forward to the time when we can have our own piano, and the girls are playing that and a couple of violins, or something.

Looks as if we're going to 4th Phase as scheduled. Hope we get the 6 days leave as planned also.

I wonder how Sylvia Madell is doing? I'll bet she's really beginning to "blossom out"—she sure is a pretty baby. What do April and Cherry K. think of her now? I just wonder if April realizes she's their new sister?

Sure wish I were there with you—there's so much we could plan together. Guess we'll get around to it later.

I just happened to think of something the girls would have lots of fun doing, and they could do some work, too. They could stick pecans in the ground out at the farm, and someday we'd have plenty of pecan trees. I'll do that with them next time I come home.

I hope you can get a girl to work for you in the house after the nurse leaves. I certainly want you to take a long rest this time.

Kiss all three of our sweet girls for me. I'm the richest man in the whole world, far richer than I ever dreamed I'd be—to have three beautiful daughters and a lovely wife. I love you so much, my Darling.

C. L.

February 16, 1943

Dearest Sweetheart,

I'm glad you can remember dates. I didn't remember what date I proposed to you, but it gives me a thrill to recall it now. I was just as much thrilled as you were, and probably scared twice as badly; maybe that's why I can't remember much about it—I was in such a daze. I don't know why most men get buck fever at a time like that; but I've heard they all do.

I've been talking tonight with some officers back from the Southwest Pacific. They sure have had some experiences. They were in the same outfit with Jack Carlson and all rate him as the best navigator and intelligence officer in that Group. He's coming through here tomorrow. I'm going to talk to him if he's here long enough.

O, I surely would like to see you and the girls tonight. I miss you so much, but am happy as a pig in the sunshine in just having you and knowing we should be together again shortly. I don't have any idea where I'm going, but I imagine it will be a permanent static group somewhere—probably as a group Executive. I doubt that I'll get a group of my own as there are too many young regular army Lieutanent Colonels running around that they have to take care of. That suits me fine, but I'd sure like to get a promotion.

Kiss the little girls for me, especially the one with the dimples. I've got a lot of loving to do to catch up on Madell. Tell her that Daddy will make up for lost time when we're together again.

I love you so, Darling—Goodnight.

      Your devoted husband

CHAPTER NINE
MAN WITH A MISSION

Spring brought some lovely things. C. L. now stationed in Topeka, Kansas, received his promotion to Lieutenant Colonel and wrote, asking us to meet him in San Antonio for two wonderful days before he left to take his crew to North Africa via South America. He expected to be gone only a month, after which he hoped we could be settled again together for awhile.

C. L. was so handsome in his uniform bearing his new insignia—silver oak leaves. My heart swelled with joy—I was so proud of him—proud of his accomplishments, his patriotism, his noble Christian principles and clean living. As his plane rose into the fair Texas sky, the girls and I waved until there was only a speck visible.

> This will
> Bring a rent, too,
> In my heart when you go
> But the Master Mender knows that
> He heals
> —Mada Scott

Wednesday Night

Dearest Sweetheart,

I'm in the middle of the packing again. Looks like I'd get used to this, but it always takes as long or longer than it did last time I packed. I'm having my footlocker sent home as it's too heavy to take. Just stow it anywhere until I get back.

This came as a surprise. We weren't expecting to leave this soon. We'll probably get away for Florida sometime tomorrow, and get a good rest before starting from there. I would get caught like this with practically all my clothes dirty and too late to take them to the cleaners. Guess I'll keep wearing them like that.

I cashed a check for $50 here today to take on the trip. I'll try to arrange at Morrison Field to have my pay check sent to the bank at the end of the month. (They wouldn't do it here for some reason or other.) If I can't do that, I'll cable it to you—unless I get back here before the 10th of next month. You'll have enough until then with just the allotment.

I've got to finish this packing or I'd write more. I'm still all thrilled at having been with you the two days at San Antonio. I love you and the little girls so much, Darling, and am the happiest guy in the world in just knowing I have you.

I know your prayers are always with me, Dearest. Mine are with you, too, for I worry (or rather try not to worry) about you and the girls. But I guess you can take care of yourself pretty well as far as sickness is concerned.

Will write on the way as I have a chance now

and then. As April says, "Be back!" Bless her little heart.

All my love,
C. L.

P.S. I apparently will have no forwarding address. If I do, will let you know later. I'll beat the letters back anyway.

Saturday Night, March 20

My Darling Wife and Babies,

We finally got away from Topeka after much wrangling over technical details of loading after the weather had cleared. I've really been "rushin' around" like the rabbits in "Deep in the Heart of Texas."

Weather is holding us up to the East Coast, probably all day tomorrow, too. I called the folks [my uncle and aunt] at Beckville and am going over there to spend tomorrow with them. I sure wish you could be here, Darling. I miss you so.

My orders read that I'm coming back immediately, so I shouldn't be gone long. I can hardly wait to get back and get settled again with you and the girls.

There's a new song that I sure like—it seems to fit us—you and me—why, I don't know, but it's real pretty. It starts with the words "The bells are ringing for me and my gal" or something like that—"The birds are singing—for me and my gal," etc.

If you can get the record, I think you'll enjoy it.

Hug and kiss our baby girls for me.

All my love to my beautiful gal.

Your husband

P.S. Yes, I saw you waving after we took off. I was looking for you. I waved, too, but you couldn't see me, I'm sure.

I hope the girls are feeling better.

Before C. L. left the States, he sent the girls and me two large beautiful pieces of luggage, brown leather. They were certainly useful, for we packed them and went to stay a few weeks with Mama who was teaching at Dime Box, Texas.

Friday, March 26

My Darling Wife and Baby Girls,

It seems such a long time since I've seen you, and I'm quite a distance from you tonight but am just started.

Can't tell you where I am, when I came, or when I'm leaving—and oh, yes, the weather. All my mail is subject to censorship now.

This is a beautiful place, though. Several of us spent a few hours this evening walking along the beach and through a coconut grove.

The trip so far has been like one on the Magic Carpet—very beautiful and interesting—almost to the point of being unreal. Hope it's all like this.

I saw a little bird with a nest built in the rocks

along a wooded cliff near the beach—about the size of a little wren. I got a chance to study him closely, and it's a miniature dove. Looks exactly like a Texas mourning dove, except it's about a third as big.

The post here is very pretty. Wish you could see it.

I hope you and the girls are well, I miss you so much, Dearest. Give Mother and Dad my love. Don't know when I'll get another letter to you, maybe soon. Mail will be slow, though.

All my love to the most precious little girls and my darling sweetheart.

Your devoted husband

Sunday, March 28

My Dearest,

Again I can't tell you where I am, but I'm somewhere in South America. This is a beautiful place—plenty of jungle, tropical birds, etc. Your mother would really enjoy a visit here—there are all kinds of strange birds making stranger noises. She could probably identify some of them.

I had a sun bath today, just loafed around and rested. Everything is going fine except I miss you.

How are you and the little girls? I'd sure like to see you now. Tell them that if I ever get to go into town I'll buy them some souvenirs.

There's so much I want to tell you but of course I can't. Well, it's interesting anyway.

Went to church service today. The chaplain is

a young fellow, isn't very good as a preacher, but I enjoyed it, anyway. I wondered if you were at church, too, with the girls.
Write soon.
All my love to my four sweethearts,
C. L.

> Somewhere in Africa
> Monday, April 5

My Darling,
Don't know when you'll get this. I hope you got my cablegram. Hope you're all O.K. I'd give anything for a letter from you, but I know not to expect one for quite awhile.

I'm really enjoying this jaunt—it's so interesting, expecially in Africa. The climate suits me fine so far. I think I could completely get over the cold I've had in my chest all winter if I could get a few more days of sunshine and loafing.

Recently while on leave, I visited the Gold Coast of South Africa. Spent a couple of days swimming at the most beautiful beach I've ever seen, in the roughest surf—waves ten feet high. Also rode in a native dugout canoe with five husky natives paddling and chanting in the most peculiar language. They took us out for about 200 yards, turned around and rode an enormous wave in to the beach. We got turned sideways just before beaching and turned over in the water. It was really fun.

I also went sight-seeing at the native bazaar

Man with a Mission

(market and trading post). The old story of giving trinkets, beads, etc., to the native is wrong—they sell them to the white men, and how! An intensive bargaining must be gone through, usually starting by offering ¼ of what is asked for the curio. You end the deal by paying about ½ of the price asked (and you get stuck at that, as far as honest-to-goodness African trading goes). I got a few little trinkets for very little money.

I wish I had brought our movie camera along. The natives are the most colorful you can imagine. They're black as coal and nearly all fine physical specimens. Some of them are wrapped from chin to foot in gaudy-colored cloth (some solid red, some lavender, purple, light blue, and some in a dozen different colors).

Nearly all the little babies are very cute until they get about two years of age. Then their bellies usually distend. It's caused, I'm told by a surgeon, by an enlarged spleen caused by malaria. Everyone has malaria, and great precaution is taken against it. A couple of adebrine tablets are served every other day with our meals.

I watched a Mohammedan say his daily prayers—it's all public, or rather is done usually in public market places, where a prayer-ground is provided. First, he washed his hands, face, and feet with water from a common washing barrel. This took quite awhile, and he was very thorough. Then he entered the praying-plot and started his ritual, which had a definite procedure that must have taken years to memorize. Regardless of the cruelty and evil practises for which they're noted, it must be said of the Mohammedan that he evidences a more passionate belief in God than we do. His entire life, day and night hour after hour, is centered and planned around Allah—and if he feels he has fallen short of the normal requirements of his worship, he will inflict physical torture on himself for atonement. We, on the other hand, usually merely include God as the One vital necessity in our scheme of things, calling on Him for help when we need Him, often leaving our faith in the background until we frantically realize our plight. We could learn from the Mohammedan.

I said the natives had fine bodies. You should see how straight they carry themselves. It's from carrying heavy loads on their heads. They never carry any load except on top of their heads and they start early in life. Women with little babies carry them wrapped to their backs, and often a hundred pound load on their heads, yet they walk erect with an easy, swinging gait.

It's impossible for us back home to realize how great the soldier's sacrifice is when he's on foreign service during war. It's not the physical hardships—he can get used to that—but it's the longing to see his family, his hometown and things that are American instead of foreign. His greatest problem is homesickness.

It makes me feel good all over to see how Americans as a general rule get along so much better with the natives of all the places I've been, than other foreign peoples do. It must be something of our democratic principles that we're not aware of back home. It seems to be due mostly to an easy tolerance of the other man's ideas, no matter whether the other man happens to be black, dark brown, or yellow-skinned. If Hitler could conquer the entire world, he certainly couldn't keep it that way for long, although he could deal out plenty of misery while he had it.

I miss you so much, Darling, and am counting the days when I'll get to be with you and the little girls. Kiss them for me, and tell them I'll bring some presents to them.

I love you with all my heart.

C. L.

Somewhere in Africa
Thursday, April 8, 1943

My Dearest,

Herblin and I went swimming about an hour on the beach today and I got a nice sunburn, even though it was a cloudy day.

Looks as if it's going to take nearly twice the time I figured on, before I can be with you and the girls. The best part of being on this duty is looking forward to being with you, Darling. I miss you so much. I've been planning on what we're going to do when we're together. Most of the time we'll just be at home with our baby girls, but about twice a week we'll get someone to take care of the girls while we have an afternoon together playing tennis, or shopping, or just walking around on a date (like we used to do in school). Then maybe we can take the girls on a picnic out in the country about once a week. If I possibly can, I'm going to make arrangements to have plenty of time off with you, regardless of what job I'm on when I get back. I think we've been "too much married" the last few years and haven't taken the time out to be just plain sweethearts knocking around together. Whatever I do, don't let me get in the habit again of spending more time at official duties than is absolutely necessary, because overwork is as bad as neglecting a job; also because every minute I ever spent with you is a precious part of my life.

It takes something like this of getting out away from everything to make you realize that life is so very beautiful if you make it that way, and we certainly want to make the most of it when we get back together.

I'd sure like to get a letter from you to find out what's happening and if you're O.K. I ask God to take care of you constantly, and I know He will. Don't ever worry about me, for I'm perfectly safe at all times. If you don't get a letter for a couple or three weeks, think nothing of it. It's easily possible for a letter to get lost in transit, or to be delayed for quite some time.

Kiss our girls for me. I'll bet Madell will really

be flowered out into a beautiful baby when I see her. I miss you all so much, my Dearest.

All my love,
C. L.

CHAPTER TEN
BRITAIN BOUND

The spring days with Mama were enjoyable. When the girls began having various illnesses, thinking that I needed to be near a doctor, I rented a little apartment in Giddings, Texas—the town where I was born. It was only a short distance from Dime Box, so we saw Mama often. I found special solace in the simultaneous ringing of church bells on Sunday mornings there in Giddings—a comforting experience which helped dispel the thoughts of the wretchedness of war.

C. L. was gone much longer than expected. I grew restless and packed our things, deciding to return to Brownwood. I supposed he would come there first. It had been two weeks or more since I had had a letter from him. Mama understood my nervous ways, so, in early May, after fond good-byes, the girls and I drove to Brownwood.

In a few days C. L. went to Dime Box first, thinking we were there. After seeing Mama, he caught the next bus to Brownwood. Eagerly I awaited his arrival, and seeing him leave the bus, I rushed into his arms. Such a blessed time of reunion! We all could hardly contain our joy.

He was home for ten days, some of which we spent on our farm. He had brought gifts for us; one of my gifts was a star sapphire ring. Before he had to leave again, he bought the girls some clothes. One little dress he bought Madell was pale green checked; our little Texas Rose, now nearly four months old, looked so sweet dressed in green. We took some family pictures and also some of C. L. with each of the girls and with me. Just before he left, we all enjoyed a picnic together. He thought perhaps he would now have a permanent station somewhere in the States, but that was not to be. His orders directed him to England to Headquarters 402nd combat wing to be Chief of Staff for General Nathan Bedford Forrest (great-grandson of General Forrest of Civil War Days whom General Robert E. Lee termed the greatest soldier under his command).

> Tell me not, Sweet, I am unkind
> That from the nunnery of thy chaste breast and quiet mind
> To war and arms I fly.
>
> Yet this inconstancy is such
> As you, too, shall adore:
> I could not love thee, Dear,
> so much
> Loved I not honour more.
> —A 17th century Cavalier poet

New York City
Sunday P.M., May 23

My Darling,
I'm all lined up on a ride over in a big C-54 about Wednesday, with Pan-American. I decided

not to try to get a ship to ferry over as it's a lot of trouble, and a C-54 is so much more comfortable. (Guess I'm getting lazy.) This way I'll only make one stop enroute.

I was really pooped out when we got in yesterday, so instead of checking in where I was supposed to, I came on into Manhattan, got a room at a hotel, went to bed and slept until late this morning. Went out to the field today, found there was still no particular hurry (yet they had to cut my leave short), so I'll have a couple of days to look around and buy a few items I'll need later that I can't get over there. I've already picked up some more color film so I should at least have some interesting pictures when I come back. I haven't been able to find any 8mm color film for the movie camera. I wanted to send you some if I could get it.

I saw some star sapphires in a show window yesterday on Fifth Avenue. One was so large it was unbelievable. It was nearly the size of a bantam egg and had a perfect star in the exact center. It was a pale, rather dull color, though, and was too enormous to be beautiful. The price was $4,000. I saw another one with a pretty star, about ¾ the size of yours, perfectly shaped, but not as good color as yours—for $200. If I'm ever again in Cairo, I'm going to get another one—maybe one small one for each of the girls. I regret not getting them when I was there—didn't have that much money at the time.

I feel so much better knowing you're going to

have a place to settle with the girls for awhile, rather than moving from "pillar to post." If I must be off fighting in this war (I'll probably be fighting paperwork), it's much better for the girls and you to have a house you can call home until I get back.

Let's make an agreement not to worry about each other, Darling. I worry about you and the girls getting sick, or hurt, and I know you worry about my safety. The solution is so simple that we make it difficult by refusing to believe it. Human reasoning takes us only as far as the impossible. Faith takes us far beyond that into the realm of the unfathomable, and we call them miracles. Really they aren't—they're merely the guarantee of a promise: "Whatsoever ye shall ask in my Name, believing, that will ye also receive." And that promise is just as good today as it was two thousand years ago when Christ made it, time and time again, to the doubting world of mortals.

Try to get the idea over to Dad, too, if you can. He loses courage easily when things look pretty dark. Mother's not so much that way—she refuses to let her faith be shaken.

Will write some more later.

All my love to my lovely wife and babies,

C. L.

Thursday Night

My Darling,

It was wonderful hearing your voice tonight. I wish we owned part of the telephone company and could talk as long as we liked when I'm away like this, don't you? Mr. Alex Bell was a fine fellow indeed to give the world such an invention. It was good to hear Mother and the girls, too. (I never did hear April say anything. I imagine she had her nose covered with her hand puffing and blowing like a little seal.) Bless her little heart. I love them so.

I went to the Museum of Natural History today. It was really interesting. I took a roll of plain film of the wildlife exhibits there. They're really life-like and I believe will make real good pictures. I'll send you some as soon as they're developed. If I have to leave before the color slides come, I'll have them sent back to you. I'm sure anxious to see them.

I am thoroughly fed up with New York by now. Not that it isn't interesting—it is. But it's the fact that while I'm waiting for my ride over, we've got to spend all this time apart. (I wish my orders would suddenly get revoked. Maybe they will, if they decide at the other end of the line that I'm not coming.)

Here's another good suggestion on how we can keep in closer contact with each other. Am enclosing a note about *Reader's Digest*. Although we couldn't very well exchange notes by mailing the *Digest* back and forth, we could at least be thinking along the same line of thought suggested by articles each month in the *Digest*. After I get assigned to my new unit, I'll probably want you to have the *Digest* sent to me each month, unless they are available there on the newsstands, which I doubt.

I love you, my beautiful red-headed Sweetheart—you and our three lovely daughters, too. I'm the richest man that ever lived, because I've got you.

Your devoted husband

It was security for the girls and me to have the little brick home C. L. bought for us before he left for New York. The hours of several days were spent getting our rooms in order. The girls enjoyed the back yard; they had a gym set to play on, and also a tepee to play in with plenty of room to make-believe.

Life was rapidly changing for many. Fred, C. L.'s youngest brother, was a pursuit pilot. His brother Irvine was in the Quartermaster Division; his brother Vernon was an officer in the Infantry. Bubba had joined the Navy and was in the Pacific theater of War. Our pastor, Dr. Moore, joined the Air Force as chaplain. Hearts were rended in many homes as parting with loved ones seemed inevitable.

Getting to talk with C. L. by telephone before he left New York was certainly a treat. He sent gifts to us: a music box for each of the girls; a music box for me and also a riding habit (to wear riding on our horse farm). He had some excellent studio pictures made of himself, having the studio send to us after he left New York.

The summer days were filled with working

around the house and playing with the girls. We were able to get established in church here and went regularly, enjoying the preaching of the Word and the warm fellowship of First Baptist.

We looked forward to C. L.'s letters from England; we wrote to him, and also sent him packages—items he needed and could use. After praying for him I was also comforted to hear the girls pray for "Dear Daddy."

June 10, 1943
England

Dearest Sweetheart,

For the first time since I've been here I'm taking the time out to write you a letter instead of a short note. I doubt if you got my other letters because they were in the wrong kind of V-mail; if it's sealed, I'm told it goes by boat and takes much longer. I had some work to do at the office tonight which makes it convenient to write you. There's no light in my quarters but there is here. I don't expect any mail from you for a couple of weeks yet, because we've had to move around so much, so my first letter from you will really be a thrill.

Lt. Colonel Hank Celik is here. He's the same old Hank and hasn't changed a bit. We were glad to see each other. Also many of the boys who were at Sebring are here, including my former co-pilot, South. He's a veteran now, having several raids under his belt. (Anyone who's been on one raid, though, is a veteran, for the simple reason that you couldn't be scared any more than you were on that first one, so they tell me.)

I didn't think I could possibly work as hard with a thousand details daily, without much sleep, as I'm doing now, and still keep healthy; but I've got a ravenous appetite all the time and believe I'm gaining weight. Guess it's the climate.

Hon, the first chance you get I'd like you to send me a couple of boxes of No-Doz tablets. There will be times that I'll have to work all night without any sleep and they're good at keeping the mind clear without any bad after-effects. That shouldn't be very often that I need them.

I'd give anything to see you, Darling, and our precious girls. I'll pretend you're just over in the next village, instead of across a lot of water.

Have been driving around some in rural districts here. The farmhouses are made of stone with thick roofs of straw. The fields are small, with tall green grass or grain that looks like a farmer's dream. The horses here are all big draft type with long shaggy hair on their feet. Everything is picturesque in the country; old churchhouses with cemeteries showing tombstones hundreds of years old. I enjoy driving over to the various bases because I get to see the part of England that's really worth seeing.

I've got to get a little sleep in, Hon. Will try

to get a longer letter off to you later. Goodnight. All my love to my darling wife and babies.

C. L.

June 13, 1943

My Darling,

Today being Sunday, I spent the day buried in work as usual. Boy, I'll really be glad when this mess is cleaned up and we can resume normal life. There's a big job to do here, though, and I'm glad I'm qualified to do my part of it. It's mostly training other people, and I got plenty of that back home. I thought I had quit writing directives when I left, but apparently have just started. Good old paperwork war! That's the only way to get it over, so everyone understands, I guess. I missed going to church today; hope I can go next Sunday. I don't miss any praying, though. God is a very real necessity here, just as I've been told by other people back from the combat theater. There's something different here from back home. Whether you're fighting or training, you're in some way made to realize that America must fight and pray her way through this war and that we're learning a great moral lesson brought on by adversity. We can never again afford to be lazy, neither in a spiritual nor a physical sense.

Have been doing some flying around lately in a little Piper cub; first time I ever flew one. It's lots of fun and I can study the details of all the farms, since it's so slow. This is sure pretty country here.

Hope you and our babies are well and getting organized again in our new home. I miss you so much, but that will make the homecoming so much sweeter, when I get back.

All my love, Darling,
C. L.

June 16, 1943
England

Dearest Sweetheart:

Have just been looking at some pictures of you and the babies. I'm almost afraid to look at them because I get so all-fired homesick when I do, but they look awfully sweet to me. I've been so much at my job lately that I'm getting tired of it and long for something plain, simple, and peaceful. Today I caught myself singing "Over the River and Through the Woods to Grandfather's House We Go," etc. Hank Celik looked at me like he thought I was nutty. Maybe I am at that, but I can see a bunch of wild poppies, a bird, or a big pheasant in a field near here, and momentarily forget what's going on over here. I don't have to go on these missions but I think it's more difficult to plan them for the boys who do, and meet them as they return (some of them don't return occasionally). I wish our people at home could understand the sacrifice their boys are making here; I'm sure they don't realize it except in a hazy way. Now that my C.O. is gone, I'm temporarily commanding the Headquarters, and have my hands full! Hope they send another one in soon. My greatest strength is in reading my Bible; I'm glad you got it for me. These forts don't carry any armor plates as strong as that Book is. It can stand off a 20 mm. shell from an enemy fighter when nothing else can.

I still haven't got any mail from you, but suppose it will come eventually. I've moved several times since I came here. I wonder how you are and pray you are all right. Love our baby girls for me, and a kiss to you for each mile that separates us. Give my love to Mother and Dad; I hope they're well. You're the most wonderful woman in the world, my Darling.

Your husband,
C. L.

July 3, 1943
England

My Darling,

I've been so glad to get your several letters lately. They really started rolling in and I'm sorry I haven't found more time to send you as many. I'm in a rather bad spot at present. As you know from reading the papers, General Forrest was shot down on a raid, and I've been put under a new C.O.—and we're not exactly of the best accord.

The situation will straighten itself out eventually, I hope, although I don't know how. Frankly, I'm looking for a new place to hang my hat. Oh, well. . . .

The pictures came, Darling. Thanks a million for them. I have them mounted on my dresser mirror and I look at you and our girls each time I turn around, and I love you a hundred times more than I ever thought was possible. I'm so proud of you all, and am eager to accept the many fine compliments the Staff passed on you. So as David says, "My cup runneth over." God has blessed us so and I'm thankful to Him.

I got all your letters at once about Cherry K. breaking her arm, and up to the time when she was finally O.K. It hurt me because she was hurt, but I'm glad you told me. Bless her sweet little heart, our little girl is growing up, and I know she has hard knocks to take, but I hope they'll not be too hard for her. April must be sweeter and prissier every day. I wish I could see her. And I can hardly believe Madell is almost crawling.

I'll send you some pictures next letter. I hope I can write you several letters soon. I'm awfully busy now at night at the office and get little time off.

It's after 1:00 A.M. and I must turn in awhile. All my love to my Sweetheart and Baby girls.

Your husband

England,
July 6, 1943

My Darling,

Your cable came today. It gave me a start at first, but was glad to get it. I'm sure that you have a letter from me by now acknowledging your other letters. The mailman has really been good to me lately. I got four letters one day and eight day before yesterday. I don't know where to start answering them. I'm not kidding when I say I'm getting the honk worked out of me, even though I'm not flying on missions at present.

I'd give anything to see you and the girls, Hon. It's a good thing I'm not idle here or I'd really bemoan being here. It's at night when I look at your pictures and read your letters that I really want to be there. I've begun to develop a passive attitude about the whole thing, though, for I realize I've got to stay here just so long (how long I don't know), and when that time is up, I go home. So each night sees another day scratched off, and I try to and do get some satisfaction out of that. Please don't feel bad about our being separated, Darling, if you can help it. I know it's bad for our babies to be without me for so long, but it would be much worse if they had to be without you instead of me. I very distinctly remember the saddest part of my life as a kid was when I had to be away from both Mother and Dad. Just keep them thinking of me, and I know they do. (Bless their little hearts.)

There's so much I can't tell you because of censorship. It's a big show, though, if not the biggest. I've seen things happen that seem now like something in the movies they were so unreal. At first I was scared stiff, or rather so excited and scared I could hardly control myself. Since then I was merely excited, but quite able to think clearly. One thing that is quite clear to me is the fact that we can win this war quickly if we have faith in God. Anyone can do anything if his faith is strong enough. I've actually seen it put to test—not once, but several times. And I'm rather optimistic about the whole outlook for us, same as the newspapers are.

Am sending some pictures Lt. Reese made of some of us. I haven't got any of the color pictures back that I sent in to be developed here.

I suppose Dr. Moore felt his place was with our forces, but I'm sorry to see him go. Probably (in my opinion) he could do as much by staying at home with his family. I wish I were there now.

All my love to my dearest wife and baby girls. I love you, Darling, with all my heart.

C. L.

. . . . .

In a letter to his brother Irvine, C. L. wrote the following: "Our boys are doing a swell job. You can't tell me that the American youth isn't the finest in the world. He may at times be a rugged individualist, but he gets the toughest job done in a manner to be commended."

July 8, 1943
England

My Dearest,

I'll get off a line to you while I'm on duty tonight. My work at night is not at all difficult, but just mostly requires my presence. (In other words, I'm being paid for what I know rather than for what I do. Soft job, hey?)

I just received your letter (June 7) with the picture. I really enjoy the pictures, and have quite an art gallery in my quarters. All my girls are around me every time I go to my room, and it seems that you're really there with me. I only wish you were.

Sure wish I could see our new home. I know it must be attractive. I'm really looking forward to coming home on leave. I'm going to ask for 30 days when I come back. Yes, I think you ought to set out some pecan trees there. A little later on, after I've paid back the money to the finance office, I'll send you money monthly (about $200, I think). I'm getting by here on $100 monthly, and am sure my expenses won't run over that amount. Then you can get that lot next to you. That place will make us a nice permanent home.

Yes, I went to church, or rather chapel, on the 27th, although it was much earlier than you did. (It was about 5:00 A.M. there when we had our services here.) I very seldom get to go, although I have the opportunity each day. We have short services everyday at 11:30.

I wonder if you had read about General Forrest. Funny thing, he flatly refused to let me go on that mission. I hope he's O.K. and I feel pretty optimistic about him. I got to know him very well and he thought lots of me in spite of my criticism of his work back in the States. We held exactly the same views which made me feel good, as I've been told my policy is too strong, or something. There's no doubt in my mind that the General is one of the greatest commanders of this war.

My old co-pilot at Sebring is an airplane commander here—Lt. South—he's quite a boy. We were glad to see each other.

Glad to get your phone number but I can't fulfill that promise of calling you from here. They've cut out that service now, so I'll have to be content with writing you.

I've gained about 5 lbs.—my clothes are too small already. Guess I'll get as big as Winston Churchill this winter. No need to send any apricot jam as we get it here. It's better to send something more concentrated like candy, or the best thing I can think of right now would be some limburger cheese. You can't get cheese here, and it's pretty good to snack on when I work late at night, which is practically every night.

Monday, July 12,

Hon,

I started this letter 4 days ago and never got a chance to finish it. I wish I could get another job that didn't take so much of my time so I could write you daily. I feel like I'm not treating you right in sending so few letters, but my time is all split up. Right now I've just finished for the day and it's the next day (1:00 A.M.). I enjoy your letters so much and look forward to them. I've received a good many, about 25 I think, and the pictures (the last 3 of the girls are really good, and I've been showing them to everyone today). Bless their precious hearts, I'd like to see them.

Hon, don't worry about my enduring any hardships here. I have the best food (even better than at Clovis). My quarters are very comfortable. I have a good bath as often as I have time to bathe (about twice a week), and the climate is refreshing all the time. I have a transformer and am using my electric razor again, have an electric heater in addition to my coal stove, and lack nothing—except being with you and the girls, which is all that matters. In spite of my long hours, I'm gaining weight and feel fine.

I took time off yesterday to go to church (Church of England—mostly Episcopal). I sat in the choir and sang with them as best I could. Their music is different and difficult. The Cathedral was very old, built in 1096. We spent some time looking it over afterward. It has Edith Cavell's grave there and scores of old Anglo-Saxons and Anglo-Normans. Some of the epitaphs are in the original Anglican language which I can't read. I also saw a castle where William the Conqueror made his headquarters after conquering England. If I ever get a day off I'm going through the castle and back through the Cathedral to see the rest of it.

My Darling, your letters are an inspiration to me. They provide complacency when everything else seems to be going wrong, and put me back on the right track again. An ocean can't begin to separate us because I seem to know when you're thinking of me, and I know you feel the same way. All my love to my dearest Sweetheart and my three little Lovelies.

C. L.

Wednesday, P.M.
July 28

My Darling,

I haven't had a chance to write you the past few days, I've been so engaged in my work. I'm getting ready to go to bed tonight as I didn't get to bed at all last night. Things come in spasmodic spurts here. I'm glad you sent the No-Doz tablets; they sure help when I have to be up like that. I have no trouble at all in sleeping when I do get the chance, though. I skipped another night Saturday, and slept 16 hours Sunday night.

I wish I could help you in fixing up our home, Dearest. I know it must be beautiful in every way. Let's hope it isn't too long before I can be back there with you and the girls.

Friday, 1:00 A.M.

Sorry I didn't have time to finish this. I have plenty of time tonight, though. We're all sitting around as usual about this time, mostly waiting rather than working. (It's good to be paid for what you know, rather than what you do.) However, I actually put in a good day's work occasionally—am sending some news clippings.

I didn't get a letter from you yesterday nor the day before, but I am expecting several today. My days here are not figured from dawn to dusk, or from midnight until noon—the dividing line is at 4:30 P.M. (when the mail comes). I look forward to that time, and each time I get your letters a new, brighter day dawns for me, just like the day when I'll get orders to return home.

Eddie Rickenbacker was here recently—gave a very inspiring talk to the crews. He remembered me from our short meeting in Dakur, and I'm sure he's met a thousand people since that time. To me he will always be one of the greatest men I've ever known; not because of his record in aviation, but because he's a great, practical Christian who has the unbelievable faith in God that we all should have, and he's telling the world about it. He told of the miracles he prayed for to happen while on the raft in the Pacific, how they actually did happen, and said he wouldn't expect us to believe his story if he didn't have eyewitnesses to it. His faith, told in his simple, rough way, is converting more people than a hundred ordained ministers might convert during their entire lifetime, and the glory of it is the fact that so many of them are people who have seldom been active church-goers. His talk here, and the apparent effect it had on his audience, is something I will never forget.

Since it's now 5:15 and I think I can sneak out and over to my quarters and "hit the sack" for a few hours' sleep, I'll say goodnight and finish this some other time when I'm not so sleepy. I've been interrupted in this letter at least a dozen times.

Give our babies a kiss each from their Daddy— and a special one for my very special Sweetheart— You!

Goodnight, Darling.

C. L.

P.S. Am enclosing a snapshot (very informal) of me in my room immediately after knocking off 16 hours of sleep. The white wool jacket is part of a flying suit, and I use it for a lounge jacket. The haircut is nothing more than the English version of our American Indian scalping. I asked for a regulation military haircut and this barber hit me like a Focke-Wulfe 190, and I was almost rendered bald before I could call for help. (That was three weeks ago, before this picture was taken.)

August 10

My Darling,

Today I got two letters from you. One of your letters was written on May 31, the other was on June 2. I didn't get to write you yesterday as I was busy all day and also all night last night, and did a little flying early this morning. I got seven hours sleep today, though, and feel O.K. It's 2:00 A.M. now (I should have dated this the 11th) but I'm not sleepy. I'm beginning to sprout feathers and can see in the dark like an owl, from this heavy, fast, night-life.

You're very flattering in all your letters. It's a good thing you can't see me with this new British haircut or you'd decide I'm not so good-looking after all. It's you who are the most lovely creature I know, my Dearest.

I don't remember writing anything about coming home on leave. If I did, I was probably wacky imagining something like that, so pay no attention to it as it's the dreaming of an unstable mind. I imagine I'll be here until I complete my tour, and I don't know how long that will be. The chaplain says we'll be home by Christmas, but my opinion on that is that the chaplain must have some inside dope that the Generals don't yet know about. He should let the General Staff know about it so they can make their plans accordingly and get the War over with.

Darling, I cabled you £50 yesterday (less fee). I figure you need it. I probably won't be able to send any next month, though, but can the month after that.

Love our precious girls for me. I'd sure love to see them and you.

Kiss them goodnight for me and I send one for you. I love you so much Dearest.

C. L.

CHAPTER ELEVEN

MORE THAN A CONQUEROR

It was later in the summer when I purposed in my heart to start tithing my allotment, giving it to our church. Then I realized that with the house expenses so heavy (having had some extra work done on it) and with buying groceries, I would not have enough to make it to the next allotment check. But I decided to give the tithe anyway. A day or so after that decision, I received the cable from C. L. with the £50 ($200.) This really clinched tithing for me. Malachi 3:10 was real! "Bring ye all the tithes into the storehouse, that there may be meat in mine house, and prove me now herewith, saith the Lord of hosts, if I will not open you the windows of Heaven, and pour you out a blessing that there shall not be room enough to receive it." It was just that the Lord had whispered to C. L. to send the money when he did.

Since April's birthday was August 2, C. L. had tried to find her a gift, but to no avail. Instead he sent her a personal cablegram, and I bought her a doll as a gift from him.

On August 21, 1943, the following telegram, which was starred, arrived from the War Department:

"I REGRET TO INFORM YOU REPORT RECEIVED STATES YOUR HUSBAND LIEUTENANT COLONEL CHURCHILL L. SCOTT, JR. MISSING IN ACTION OVER ORNBSLING, GERMANY SINCE TWELVE AUGUST IF FURTHER DETAILS OR OTHER INFORMATION OF HIS STATUS ARE RECEIVED YOU WILL BE PROMPTLY NOTIFIED"
ULIO, THE ADJUTANT GENERAL

The blood seemed to drain from my body, and trembling, I went almost immediately to prayer. The Lord sent the most glorious peace through my soul which strengthened me. And because of that sweet peace I was able to go through the days, weeks, months, and years of waiting which lay ahead.

"There is a viewless cloister room
As high as Heaven
As fair as Day;
And though my feet may join the throng,
My soul can enter in and pray.

One hearkening cannot even know
When I have crossed the threshold o'er,
But He alone who hears my prayer
Has heard the shutting of the door."
—Selected

One of my friends wrote me that I had my work cut out for me—the care of the girls. Friends and loved ones were kind. One of my former professors at Howard Payne College, Mr. Yantis Robnett, came every week for some time, bringing the girls candy, gum, or some little gift. It was he who helped me try to get word about C. L., writing and calling several places.

CLOISTER THOUGHTS

I long for you in secret places
Retracing my steps to paths of yesteryear
Perhaps I'll hear again your footsteps
Along the rocky trails in Western soil,
Or hear the echo of your call in lowly wooded hills.
Perhaps I'll hear again your voice
Among the evening vespers
And see the laughter in your eyes as shadows fall,
Or sense once more your hand clasp mine
As scarlet fingers reach across the sky.
Yes, I long for you in secret places
My heart atune to distant dreams and far-off Chapel chimes.

—Mada Scott

I wrote the War Department, the Army Air Force Headquarters, the American Red Cross, the American Embassy in Brussels, Belgium, the Burgomaster in Lommel, Belgium and the families of crew members on his B-17.

On September 14, 1943, I received the following letter from the Adjutant General
Excerpt:
"I have the honor to inform you that, by direction of the President, the Air Medal has been awarded to your husband, Lieutenant Colonel Churchill L. Scott, Air Corps, for meritorious achievement.

"Since Colonel Scott has been reported to the War Department as missing in action, the decoration will be presented to you in his absence. . . ."

Here is a portion of a letter to me received from Headquarters Army Air Forces in Washington, dated April 24, 1944:

"This is in reply to your letter of March 8, 1944, concerning your husband, Lieutenant Colonel Churchill L. Scott.

"Further information has been received indicating that Colonel Scott was a crew member of a B-17 (Flying Fortress), which departed from the British Isles on a bombardment mission to Wesserling, Germany on August 12, 1943. Full details are not available, the report indicating that while enroute to the target, your husband's plane was seen to leave the formation, east of Antwerp, Belgium, and to turn back. The report further states the time, place and circumstance surrounding the disappearance of his plane are unknown.

"We hope you will have encouraging news soon . . ."

I received several letters from crew members'

families. I learned that C. L. was either not wearing his identification tags or else they were thrown off in the crash; that the purpose of his flying on the missions was so that he might understand the problems encountered by each man in the various positions on the plane. On the mission of August 12 he was flying in the position as tail gunner. He was the first to start this technique of taking another airman's place, and I assume it was his own idea.

On August 13, 1944, I received a letter from the War Department, Adjutant General's office, an excerpt of which follows:

"Since your husband, Lieutenant Colonel Churchill L. Scott, Jr., 0–357187, Air Corps, was reported missing in action 12 August 1943, the War Department has entertained the hope that he survived and that information would be revealed dispelling the uncertainty surrounding his absence. However, as in many cases, the conditions of warfare deny us such information. The records concerning your husband show that he was a member of the crew of a B-17 aircraft (Flying Fortress) and that he participated in a heavy bombing mission to Wesseling, Germany, on 12 August 1943. The plane was struck by antiaircraft fire when it was about half-way to the target and was last seen a few miles east of Antwerp.

"Full consideration has recently been given to all available information bearing on the absence of your husband, including all records, reports and circumstances. These have been carefully reviewed and considered. In view of the fact that twelve months have now expired without the receipt of evidence to support a continued presumption of survival, the War Department must terminate such absence by a presumptive finding of death. . . . In the case of your husband, this date has been set as 13 August, 1944, the day following the expiration of twelve months absence.

"I regret the necessity for this message, but trust that the ending of a long period of uncertainty may give at least some small measure of consolation. I hope you may find sustaining comfort in the thought that the uncertainty which has surrounded the absence of your husband has enhanced the honor of his service to his country and of his sacrifice."

I was distressed but undaunted. I continued prayer and writing of letters.

Here is a portion of a letter received in September, 1944, from General Arnold, Headquarters Army Air Forces, Commanding General:

"With great regret I have learned that an official determination has been made of the death of your husband, Lieutenant Colonel Churchill LaSalle Scott, Jr., who has been missing in action since August 12, 1943, in the European Area.

"The fine military services of Colonel Scott has been brought to my attention and I am gratified to know that he was an able officer, concerned only with giving his best to his Country. An expert pilot, he executed all assignments in a manner that was an excellent example in leadership and courage for his associates, and the officers who know him well are saddened by his untimely passing. We of the Army Air Force are proud to have had him as one of us and will cherish the memory of his accomplishments . . ."

The awarding of the Purple Heart was first established by General George Washington at Newburgh, New York, on August 7, 1782.

It was later that I received the Distinguished Flying Cross given to my husband posthumously. The Citation reads:

> Lieutenant Colonel Churchill L. Scott 0357187, Air Corps, Army of the United States. For extraordinary achievement while serving as a member of the crew of a B-17 type aircraft on an important mission over enemy-occupied Europe on 12 August 1943. While assigned to the 13th Combat Bomb Wing (H) as Chief of Staff, Colonel Scott frequently participated in combat missions in various crew positions in order that he might better understand their peculiarities and problems. During the return from the target, enemy fighters severely damaged the aircraft in which Colonel Scott was serving as a gunner. The courage and devotion to duty displayed by Colonel Scott in remaining at his

position to deliver defensive fire against enemy fighters while his crew members escaped were an inspiration to all members of his command and reflect the highest credit upon himself and the Armed Forces of the United States.

Here is part of a letter I received from the American Embassy in Brussels dated December 3, 1945:
"We have just received your letter of 18 November 1945 and hope that the information contained in it will be a help in locating your husband.

"In accordance with your last letter, we have been in communication with the Burgomaster of Lommel who has been most cooperative.

"We shall not fail to inform you of any information obtained concerning your husband . . ."

Hearing that some of the crew members escaped through the Underground, some were Prisoners of War, some were killed, I still entertained hope, continuing to pray and wait. One officer wrote me that C. L. gave the order to bail out when the German fighters rushed in toward the tail section of the B-17 where he was serving as gunner. He also wrote that he saw C. L. fall, but he didn't know whether or not he left the plane.

In a letter dated 18 September 1946 to a General from another General (a copy of which was sent to C. L.'s parents), the following was written about C. L.:

"He was an eager beaver if I have ever seen one, both in regard to his work on the ground and particularly in flying. He was not the kind of lad who pushed himself into positions of responsibility and subsequent award, but was the quiet, modest, unassuming type who was always ready to do any kind of a job. He actually pestered Aaron Kessler and me daily for permission to go on missions. He felt that it was necessary for him to get a complete education in the problems of each position in the airplane prior to assuming any command responsibility. He was absolutely fearless and was just as happy in the tail or the waist as he was in the navigator's compartment or the co-pilot's seat. In addition to flying, he did most of Kessler's work in the 95th War Room which, as you will remember, was the War Room for the Wing in those days, and would stay up all night as the representative of the Wing and go on a mission without any sleep.

"On the day he was killed, we had a mission scheduled to Bonn, Germany, just south of Cologne on the Rhine. Scott obtained Kessler's permission to go on this mission and then came to me with a particular request to be assigned as tail gunner, not having flown that position before. I agreed, and assigned him to the tail position of the lead airplane, thinking that was the safest spot in the formation.

"On return from the target the group was attacked by a moderate number of fighters, result of which was the loss of only one aircraft, the lead. Cole, who evaded, told us the story. This airplane was hit, caught on fire, broke formation and subsequently exploded in midair a few seconds after Cole left the airplane. During this time, in which fighters made repeated attacks, Scott stayed at his guns, firing at the attacking aircraft and was obviously, if not killed, still firing when the aircraft exploded.

". . . his general conduct and his courage in wanting to know the job thoroughly must certainly reflect, as we say in citations, the highest credit upon himself and the United States.

"If some token of his service, such as a bronze star or a D.F.C. could be awarded at this time, I am sure it would do much to ease the sense of loss that his father and mother still sustain . . ."

The following letter written February 17, 1949, from the office of Quartermaster General by Major James F. Smith tells of American Graves Registration Command and their work:

". . . A recent radiogram received from the American Graves Registration Command in the European Area reveals that the investigation concerning your husband is still in progress, and this office will be notified of the results upon completion thereof.

"Realizing your anxiety during this long period of waiting, it is my sincere hope that conclusive information will be available in the near future."

The final official letter dated 14 June, 1949,

concerning C. L., came from the Department of the Army Office of the Quartermaster General, again written by Major James F. Smith:

"In accordance with our assurance that you would be informed of any further developments in connection with the recovery and identification of your husband's remains, I am now at liberty to advise you that this identification has been established . . .

"Official German records on file in this office record the downing of your husband's plane on 12 August 1943, 5 kilometers south of Lommel, Belgium. This report lists by name the five crew members who were killed in the crash. Another German report, however, lists only four deceased from this crash as buried in the Brustem Cemetery; Colonel Scott's name does not appear on the latter report. From the fact that the complete information from his identification tag was included on the first report, it is evident that his remains were found at the time of the crash, but, by some negligence, were not removed for burial with his crewmates.

"The remains, previously designated 'The Unknown X-5115,' now identified as those of your husband, were recovered by personnel of the American Graves Registration Service from a grave in the Brustem Cemetery marked with a cross inscribed 'Unknown 11-4-44.' From interrogation of local inhabitants, it was ascertained that these remains had been found in the woods at Lommel on 10 April 1944 and were believed to be from the plane which crashed on 12 August 1943 inasmuch as no other planes had crashed in that vicinity between 12 August 1943 and April 1944. The remains were found in the area in which survivors from your husband's plane had landed after bailing out.

"In the absence of any means of immediate identification, the remains were examined by qualified technicians in a laboratory of the American Graves Registration Service in order to obtain any and all identifying data in an effort to effect identification by other means, if possible. Based upon the following evidence, thus obtained, together with the above, the identification was established:

"A. The remains were clothed in Army Air Force officer's clothing with an Air Corps insignia on the shirt.

"B. A piece of cardboard on which was inscribed the date 12 August 1943 was found with the remains by a Belgian civilian.

"C. The estimated height of the deceased, i.e., 5′ 6⅔″, compared very favorably with your husband's recorded height of 5′ 7½″.

"D. The hair color of the deceased is in agreement with the blond hair recorded for Colonel Scott.

"E. Although several of the deceased's teeth were missing after death, the comparison of the partial chart with Colonel Scott's army dental records was not unfavorable. A more complete comparison could not be made in view of the fact that no dental records were available for your husband for the period of 15 months prior to his death. The chart of the deceased indicated a few small fillings which cannot be compared; it is believed, however, that these must have been accomplished between the time of his last examination and the date of his death. It was noted that both charts indicated the wisdom teeth extracted.

"In view of the above, the identification has been established and all records will be changed to read: 'Lt. Colonel Churchill L. Scott, Jr.' His remains are at present being held in a United States Military cemetery overseas pending instructions for final interment.

"There are enclosed informational pamphlets concerning the Return of World War II Dead Program, together with a 'Request for Disposition of Remains' form on which to indicate your wishes in this matter. Promptly upon receipt of the properly completed Disposition form, necessary action will be taken to comply with your instructions as indicated thereon.

"Permit me to extend my sincere sympathy in the loss of your husband and express the hope that you will receive some small measure of solace from the knowledge that he died an honored death in the service of his country."

Letters from some Generals, other officers, friends and loved ones came to me. Then this from President Roosevelt:

> IN GRATEFUL MEMORY OF
LIEUTENANT COLONEL CHURCHILL L. SCOTT, JR.
A.S. NO. 0-357187
>
>WHO DIED IN THE SERVICE OF HIS COUNTRY IN THE EUROPEAN AREA, AUGUST 13, 1944. HE STANDS IN THE UNBROKEN LINE OF PATRIOTS WHO HAVE DARED TO DIE THAT FREEDOM MIGHT LIVE, AND GROW, AND INCREASE ITS BLESSINGS. FREEDOM LIVES, AND THROUGH IT, HE LIVES— IN A WAY THAT HUMBLES THE UNDERTAKINGS OF MOST MEN.
>
> FRANKLIN D. ROOSEVELT
PRESIDENT OF THE UNITED STATES

Much later I received this from President Kennedy:

> *The United States of America*
>*honors the memory of*
>**Churchill L. Scott, Jr.**
>
>*This certificate is awarded by a grateful nation in recognition of devoted and selfless consecration to the service of our country in the Armed Forces of the United States.*
>
> *John F. Kennedy*
>*President of the United States*

The final resting place was selected at C. L.'s home town in Brownwood, Texas, six years after the fateful morning of August 12, 1943. Although his body lay in unknown graves, yet he was not unknown to his Lord Jesus Christ. His soul went to be with the Lord and his body awaits the Resurrection.

The heartfelt message given by Dr. Moore, our pastor who performed our wedding ceremony, was touching and precious. C. L.'s youngest brother, Fred, had been killed in France in 1944. His body had lain in state for some months, awaiting the identification of C. L.'s body. We had a double memorial service in August, 1949. The flag-draped caskets, the planes flying overhead, the 21-gun salute followed by a soldier playing taps on a trumpet, reminded me afresh of that Day when the trumpet will sound and the dead in Christ will rise first.

SEALED LOVE

Sealed for Eternity
Love fresh and young
When Christ took you
So young, so brave, so true
And left me here
A few days more
That our love might
   Mature in Heaven
Sealed forever—freshly bright.

More Than a Conqueror

Eons may come and go
Swift the fleeting days
Yet our love remains untouched
Sealed in Heaven's Golden Chambers
Pure as the day
When God made you mine
Fresh as the glow of our
Hearts entwined.
—Mada Scott

When I stood at the grave of the Unknown Soldier in Washington, D.C., somehow I felt a kinship with all those who have known sorrow in War. The waving of Old Glory, the singing of the "Battle Hymn of the Republic" and thousands of other Christian mores keep always close in my heart the memory of my beloved C. L. whose steadfast desire was to serve his Lord and his country even unto death.

IMMORTAL YOU

You went away, yet now I know
    you are not gone;
You were too much of me to
    cease from living on;
Too much a part of my eternity
To be taken by mere destiny.
You went away, the mortal
    one I knew.

Still you are here, the dear
   immortal you
Who held my soul high
   in your open hand
Then clasped it close and
   watched it expand

Until it reached your soul,
   became implanted there,
Diffused itself so well no
   force could tear
The two apart. Not even death
   could separate
The two of us insensate.
      —Edythe Brehn

E'en in death I will not bind my soul in grief;
   Death cannot long divide
For is it not as though the
   rose that climbed my garden wall
Has blossomed on the other side?
   Death doth hide
   But not divide
Thou art but on Christ's other side!
Thou art with Christ and Christ with me,
in Christ united still are we.
      —Selected

EPILOGUE

How I thank the Lord for being so faithful all these years! He did what He said in Luke 24:15, "Jesus Himself drew near and went with them." Christ was there all the time.

Mama went to be with the Lord Christmas morning, 1955. Bubba was killed in a car wreck two years later. Irvine and Vernon, C. L.'s brothers, returned from the war with many unseen scars. C. L.'s dad died some years ago and his mother lives in a home for the elderly in Brownwood, Texas.

Cherry, April, and Madell were all saved early and the Lord gave them many honors in school. Each one was valedictorian of her graduating class. All have such musical ability that they have continued using for the Lord's honor and glory—singing, playing the piano and organ, and composing songs. Their other talents, too, are many. I thank the Lord for letting the girls all graduate from college.

And God must have smiled warmly when He sent each of the girls a preacher husband who could sing so beautifully with them.

The grandchildren—all eleven of them (four grandsons and seven granddaughters; and now I have great-grandchildren)—are being brought up in the nurture and admonition of the Lord—saved—have musical abilities and other gifts that the Lord gave them.

After giving me the privilege of teaching young children for twenty years, the Lord directed me to Tennessee Temple University where I have been teaching several years, training Christian teachers. How I thank Him for this and praise Him that many of our Christian teachers are serving Him faithfully in many parts of the world, witnessing and teaching children in the Way of the Lord.

And so there are many stars in my twilight of sorrow and I've been guided through the twilight by Christ, the Bright and Morning Star, Who will come for His own one day. How glorious to know we will be like Him and be forever with Him and our beloved ones. Then He will tell us why He has led us so.

"For My thoughts are not your thoughts, neither are your ways My ways, saith the Lord.

"For as the heavens are higher than the earth so are My ways higher than your ways, and My thoughts than your thoughts." Isaiah 55:8, 9.

I had secretly hoped that maybe after the war the Lord would call C. L. to preach or into the field of church music as he was a gifted musician. The Lord answered that request by multiplying C. L.'s ministry in the lives of his daughters, their husbands and their children.

"Verily, verily I say unto you, except a corn

of wheat fall into the ground and die, it abideth alone: but if it die, it bringeth forth much fruit." John 12:24.

> The latticed window
> Shown with amber light
> As looking through the
>   jeweled crevice
> I beheld your sepulcher
>   On a starlit night.
>
> I leaned closer still
> To hear the glistening sound
> Of a thousand music notes
> That dropped like dew
>   Upon the glowing ground.
>
> Notes of music so rare
>   And rhythmically alined
> Of those who follow
>   you with musicality
> My heart was tuned to
>   hear the melody refined
>
> O, God is love
> O, God is kind
> That He should choose your
>   sepulcher
> To be covered thus
>   with Angelic song
> Of those you left behind.
>   —Mada Scott